诗仙李白民间传说故事集萃
（英汉对照）

毛 若　王林莉
甘成英　毛晓红　主编
王美凤　副主编

电子科技大学出版社
University of Electronic Science and Technology of China Press
·成都·

图书在版编目（CIP）数据

诗仙李白民间传说故事集萃：英汉对照 / 毛若等主编；王美凤副主编. -- 成都：成都电子科大出版社，2025.1. -- ISBN 978-7-5770-1390-9

Ⅰ.I277.3

中国国家版本馆CIP数据核字第2024FB3902号

诗仙李白民间传说故事集萃（英汉对照）
SHIXIAN LIBAI MINJIAN CHUANSHUO GUSHI JICUI（YINGHAN DUIZHAO）

毛　若　王林莉　甘成英　毛晓红　主　编

王美凤　副主编

策划编辑	蒋　伊　唐祖琴
责任编辑	蒋　伊
责任校对	赵倩莹
责任印制	梁　硕

出版发行　电子科技大学出版社
　　　　　成都市一环路东一段159号电子信息产业大厦九楼　邮编　610051
主　　页　www.uestcp.com.cn
服务电话　028-83203399
邮购电话　028-83201495

印　　刷　成都久之印刷有限公司
成品尺寸　170mm×240mm
印　　张　10.25
字　　数　180千字
版　　次　2025年1月第1版
印　　次　2025年1月第1次印刷
书　　号　ISBN 978-7-5770-1390-9
定　　价　61.50元

版权所有　侵权必究

前　言

千百年来，中华民族祖先口耳相传流传下来很多故事，这些都是中华优秀传统文化的载体。我们既要学习历史上哲人、作家写下或流传下来的经典作品，也应了解人们口耳相传流传下来的民间故事。在我国历代诗人中，恐怕没有哪一位能像李白那样留下许多和他相关的美丽动人的民间传说故事。它们广为流布，为人乐道，有的还成为后世文学创作的题材，以致在今日的电影或电视屏幕上不时看到李白的形象。研究这些民间传说故事，揭示其真实意义，可以使我们进一步加深对李白其人其诗的认识，并从新的角度认识中国传统文化。好故事要有灵魂，好故事要有温度，好故事要有气场。《诗仙李白民间传说故事集萃（英汉对照）》不仅向我们讲述了诗仙李白成功的事实，而且更重要的是展示了诗仙李白奋斗的历程，展现了诗仙李白在失败和挫折中所表现出的杰出品质，从中我们可以吸取一些有益的精神元素。中国故事和中华优秀传统文化是中华民族的突出优势，是中华民族自强不息、团结奋进的重要精神支撑，是我们最深厚的文化软实力。

《诗仙李白民间传说故事集萃（英汉对照）》的编写具有以下几个特点。

一是人物全面。本书精心搜集、选择、编写了30个被广为传颂的有关诗仙李白的民间传说故事，这些民间传说故事和李白一生的生平事迹紧密相连，从出生、读书、游历、入京直到去世，均有传说故事萦绕。

二是角度新颖。本书不是简单地堆砌诗仙李白的材料，而是选取诗仙李白富有代表性或趣味性的故事，以点带面，从而折射出诗仙李白波澜壮阔、充满传奇的人生。这些民间传说故事大都能充分展示出李白的个性特色，包括他的天赋才华、他的飘逸风采、他的傲岸精神、他的潇洒个性。

三是篇幅适当。本书约20万字，线索清晰、语言简洁、可读性强，可用作学生的理想课外读物。

四是一书多用。本书是一部精彩的诗仙李白民间传说故事集萃，涉及三个不同的李白，即历史人物中的李白、诗歌形象中的李白和传说故事中的李白。本书能够极大地开阔青少年的视野，同时还可以作为中小学生的写作素材库。

五是中英文双语对照阅读。本书中英文双语对照阅读，可以帮助共建"一带一路"国家和地区的来华留学生了解中国历史文化，并通过阅读亲身感受中华优秀传统文化的无穷魅力。在中国"一带一路"倡议下，与中国经济交往活跃的国家来华留学生人数呈现稳定增长态势，中华优秀传统文化受到共建"一带一路"国家来华留学生的青睐，他们对中国历史文化产生了浓浓的兴趣。加强留学生的双向往来，尤其是加强共建"一带一路"国家来华留学生的中华优秀传统文化培养教育势在必行。加强共建"一带一路"国家文化交流与合作，讲好中国故事，努力传播当代中国的价值观念，展示中华优秀传统文化的当代魅力和世界影响力，突出"亲、诚、惠、容"的理念，有助于破解西方文化中心主义的干扰，消解意识形态差异造成的障碍。相信《诗仙李白民间传说故事集萃（英汉对照）》能为共建"一带一路"国家青年之间、来华留学生之间构建友谊的桥梁做出积极贡献。

值得一提的是，除作者搜集整理的故事文本外，本书还从众多脍炙人口的经典故事中认真精选，也广泛地征求了资深学者和民间文化人的意见，还从各种较好的版本中选出了最具有代表性的故事。同时，本书部分李白诗歌的译文选自许渊冲先生的翻译，谨此向这些故事的原编者和整理者以及翻译者表示真诚的感谢，并向他们致敬！如有不周到之处，敬请大家理解和谅解。由于作者水平有限，本书译文可能还存在着不少纰漏，恳请各位专家和读者不吝赐教。

毛 若

2024年12月于西南科技大学

目 录

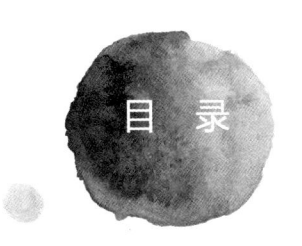

1 李白诞生蜀中的美丽故事 …………………………………1
2 洁白李花与李白名字由来的故事 …………………………6
3 "铁杵磨针"启蒙少年李白的故事 …………………………8
4 李白初露头角吟诗惊四座的故事 …………………………13
5 李白续诗辛辣讽刺县令的故事 ……………………………18
6 李白漫游蜀中驯养禽鸟的故事 ……………………………23
7 李白辞蜀远游的故事 ………………………………………33
8 李白洞庭葬友的故事 ………………………………………36
9 李白江陵幸遇司马承祯的故事 ……………………………39
10 李白拜谒李邕的故事 ………………………………………47
11 李白被称为"天上谪仙人"的故事 …………………………52
12 李白白兆山"洗脚塘"的故事 ………………………………59
13 李白白兆山"下马桩"的故事 ………………………………61
14 诗仙李白与酒的故事 ………………………………………63
15 李白黄鹤楼搁笔的故事 ……………………………………73
16 李白金陵"跳月"的故事 ……………………………………79
17 李白与"骗子"汪伦的故事 …………………………………81
18 李白沉香亭畔醉填《清平调》的故事 ………………………85

001

19	李白醉写番书的故事	92
20	李白蔑视权贵的故事	99
21	"铁杆粉丝"追星李白三千里的故事	103
22	李白骑驴过华阴县衙的故事	106
23	海上钓鳌客李白的故事	110
24	诗仙李白与诗圣杜甫相会的故事	113
25	李白与"太白酒"的故事	123
26	"太白酒家"的故事	129
27	李白投宿五松山下的故事	137
28	李白晚年求师的故事	139
29	李白大义营救郭子仪的故事	145
30	李白"千秋万岁名"称号的故事	147

Contents

1	The Beautiful Legend of Li Bai's Birthplace—Shu	3
2	White Plum Flowers and the Origin of Li Bai's Name	7
3	The Story of "Grinding an Iron Rod into a Needle" and Young Li Bai	10
4	Li Bai Shocks Audience with His Shining Poetic Talents	15
5	Li Bai Satirizes the County Magistrate with Poems	20
6	Li Bai Travels around and Domesticates Birds in Shu	27
7	Li Bai Travels Faraway outside Shu	34
8	Li Bai Buries His Friend beside the Dongting Lake	37
9	Li Bai Fortunately Meets Sima Chengzhen in Jiangling	43
10	Li Bai Visits Li Yong	49

11	Li Bai, Known as the "Demoted Immortal"	55
12	Li Bai and the "Foot-Bathing Pond" near Mount Baizhao	60
13	Li Bai and the "Dismounting Stake"	62
14	Li Bai and Wine	67
15	Li Bai Lays Down His Pen at the Yellow Crane Tower	75
16	Li Bai "Jumps into the Moon" in Jinling	80
17	Li Bai and "Liar" Wang Lun	82
18	Li Bai Drunkenly Writes *The Beautiful Lady Yang* at Chenxiang Pavilion	88
19	Li Bai Drunkenly Answers a Credential	95
20	Li Bai Despises Bigwigs	101
21	A Die-Hard Fan Chases Li Bai for Three Thousand *Li*	104
22	Li Bai Passes Huayin County *Yamen* Riding a Donkey	108
23	The Fisherman Li Bai	111
24	Immortal Poet Li Bai Meets Saint Poet Du Fu	117
25	Li Bai and "Taibai Wine"	125
26	The Story about "Tai Bai Wineshop"	132
27	Li Bai Spends One Night at the Foot of Mount Five Pines	138
28	Li Bai Seeks Teacher in His Twilight Years	142
29	Li Bai Heroically Rescues Guo Ziyi	146
30	The Origin of the Title "Long Live the Name Li Bai"	149

1 李白诞生蜀中的美丽故事

金星在我国古代被称为"太白",早上出现在东方时又叫启明、晓星、明星,傍晚出现在西方时也叫长庚、黄昏星。由于它非常明亮,最能引起富于想象力的中国古人的幻想,因此我国有关它的传说也就特别多。

在我国本土宗教道教中,太白金星可谓是核心成员之一,论地位仅在三清(太上老君、元始天尊、通天教主)之下。最初道教的太白金星神是位穿着黄色裙子,戴着鸡冠,演奏琵琶的女神,明朝以后形象变化为一位童颜鹤发的老神仙,经常奉玉皇大帝之命监察人间善恶,被称为"西方巡使"。在我国古典小说中,多次出现太白金星的传奇故事,可见他的人气之旺。在名著《西游记》中,太白金星是个多次和孙悟空打交道的好老头。

在与金星相关的众多传说中,最具有传奇色彩的应该算是关于唐代大诗人李白的故事了。唐朝大诗人李白在中国家喻户晓,但这位被誉为"诗仙"的传奇诗人究竟诞生何地呢?

李白(701—762年),字太白,号青莲居士,又号"谪仙人",是唐代伟大的浪漫主义诗人,被后人誉为"诗仙"。李白虽然是名满世界的大诗人,影响如同雨果之于法兰西,莎士比亚之于英格兰,普希金之于俄罗斯,但是由于生前没有人为他树碑立传,他自己也没有写过翔实的自传,因此对于李白的身世家世,至今仍存在着很多谜团。他的出生地、他的家世渊源、他的婚姻生活、他的后人身归何处等问题,都成为后世不断言说之谜,这也使他的人生充满了传奇色彩。

事实上,从唐代开始,对李白的诞生地就有了五花八门的说法。关于李白诞生地,众说纷纭,其中有两种说法最为集中,即一个是李白诞生于中亚西域的碎叶城(今属吉尔吉斯斯坦),另一种说法是李白诞生于四川绵阳江油的青莲乡。学术界进行了认真的考证,认同李白"出生于蜀中说"

依据最为充足。最近30年来，在四川绵阳江油出土了不少国家一级珍贵文物，也为李白诞生于四川绵阳江油青莲乡提供了佐证。

而今，李白诞生四川绵阳江油的观点已为海内外大多数学人所接受。新版《简明大不列颠全书》《中国大百科全书》有关李白的条目，都明确地表述李白是四川绵阳江油人，《中国历史》中也描述"李白，字太白，彰明人"（彰明即四川绵阳江油）。

关于李白的诞生，有一个美丽的传说在四川绵阳江油传了一代又一代，而且还载入了《四川总志》《龙安府志》《江油县志》《彰明县志》。据《江油县志》记载，701年农历正月十六日，建造了中国诗歌莽莽昆仑的唐代伟大浪漫主义诗人李白诞生在西蜀绵州昌隆（今四川绵阳江油）的青莲陇西院。因为李白祖籍在甘肃的陇西，所以他的故居就叫陇西院。李白的族叔李阳冰的记载是最有说服力的，李阳冰的《唐李翰林草堂集序》字数不多，但记写李白的诞生却用了较多的文字："惊姜之夕，长庚入梦，故生而名白，以太白字之。世称太白之精，得之矣。"《四川总志》云："龙安府平武县有蛮婆渡，在江油市青莲坝。相传李白母浣纱于此，有鱼跃入篮内。烹食之，觉有孕，是生白。"

这个关于李白诞生的美丽故事是这样的：

太白金星被玉皇大帝贬下凡尘，出得南天门，来到西蜀的青莲乡，但见此地山明水秀，竹木茂盛，田土肥美，如人间仙境，决定在此投生。时见一端庄秀气的妇女在盘江河边浣纱，就摇身变成一尾金色鲤鱼，向江边游去，冲开纱线，跳进竹篮。这妇女正是李白的母亲，她和丈夫刚来这里不久，见鲤鱼跳入自己篮中，又惊又喜，当晚与丈夫一起烹食，便觉有了身孕。怀胎十月，李白的母亲做了一个很奇怪的一梦。她到底梦见了什么呢？原来，她梦到了一片很美丽的星空。那么多闪亮的星星都在冲她眨眼睛呢，实在让人有些看不过来了。不过，还是有一颗很特别的星星吸引了李白母亲的注意。这是秋天傍晚西方天边上最早升起的那颗最亮的星，叫作太白金星，也就是我们今天所说的启明星。它是那么耀眼那么闪亮，把夜空中其他的星星一下子就比下去了。正当李白的母亲抬着头望着这颗太白金星赞叹它的明亮耀眼时，这颗太白金星忽然从天而降，恰巧落入了李白母亲的怀里。这时，李白的母亲感到肚子一阵疼痛。于是，一个白白胖胖的小生命便呱呱落地了。因为这个太白金星的梦，李白的父亲母亲便决定给他们可爱的儿子起名李白，字太白，长大后的李白也确有几分"仙气"。

1 The Beautiful Legend of Li Bai's Birthplace—Shu

Venus was called Tai Bai in ancient China, which is also called Morning Star when it appears in the east in the morning, and Evening Star in the west in the evening. Because of its brightness, it aroused great imagination of ancient Chinese people and there are many legends about it.

In Taoism, the local religion in China, Tai Bai is one of the core members, whose status is just next to the Sanqing (the three highest gods of Taoism: Yuqing, Shangqing and Taiqing). Before the Ming Dynasty, Tai Bai of Taoism was imaged as goddess dressed in a yellow skirt, wearing a cockscomb and playing *pipa*. After the Ming Dynasty, this god was imaged as an old celestial being with a young face and white hair, and was called "patrol from the western paradise", supervising the world of good and evil under the order of the Jade Emperor. Tai Bai was so popular that his legends were repeatedly told in classical fictions. For example, Tai Bai, a kind geezer in the famous classic *Journey to the West*, often makes contact with Sun Wukong (one of the main characters).

Among those numerous legends associated with Venus, the most legendary one is about Li Bai, the great poet in the Tang Dynasty. But where was this widely known poetic genius born?

Li Bai (701—762 A.D.), whose stylistic name was Tai Bai, or literally "Great White", a reference to the planet Venus, is also referred to as Buddhist Qinglian (a pseudonym) and the "Demoted Immortal". He is regarded as a great romantic poet in the Tang Dynasty. Although he is such an outstanding poet of the world whose influence to China is what Hugo's to France or Shakespeare's to England, or Pushkin's to Russia, there have never been any monuments built for him or any detailed biographies written about him. Therefore, there are a lot of mysteries about his birth and his family. His birthplace, his family origin, his marriage, his life, his posterity and other issues, have also become mysteries for later generations.

In fact, there have been a number of stories about the birthplace of Li Bai since the Tang Dynasty. His birthplace has sparked off many debates, which can be divided into two main theories. One is that he was born in Suyab (present Kyrgyzstan) that belongs to the western mid-Asia. The other is that he was born in Qinglian town, Jiangyou of Mianyang city, Sichuan province, China. According to academic research, there is evidence that Li Bai was born in the Shu Region, which is in the southwest of ancient China. In the last 30 years, many precious cultural relics have been found in Jiangyou. These findings also provide enough evidence for the theory that Li Bai's birthplace is in Qinglian town.

Now, the latter view that Li Bai was born in Jiangyou has been accepted by most scholars all over the world, which is also clearly stated in the new edition of *Concise Encyclopedia Britannica* and *Encyclopedia of China*. *The Chinese History* also writes: "Li Bai, whose stylistic name was Tai Bai, was born in Zhangming (Jiangyou, Mianyang city, Sichuan province)."

There is a beautiful legend about the birth of Li Bai, and it has been passed down from generation to generation and finally was written into *Sichuan Records*, *Long An Government Records*, *Jiangyou County Records* and *Zhangming County Records*. According to *Jiangyou County Records*, on January 16th of the Chinese calendar, 701 A.D., Longxi Garden of Qinglian town was built in Changlong county, Mianzhou city, West Shu (present Jiangyou, Mianyang city, Sichuan province). It was the birthplace of Li Bai, the great romantic poet of the Tang Dynasty. Because his ancestral home was in Longxi, Gansu province, his former residence was called Longxi Garden. The record in Li Yangbing's work is more convincing. Although there were a few words in *The Preface to Cottage of Hanlin Li Collection*, most of them were about the birth of Li Bai. "As the story goes to the story, one night before his birth, Li Bai's mother dreamed of Venus, so Tai Bai became Li Bai's stylistic name. And people regarded him as the reincarnation of Venus." According to *Sichuan Records*, "Li Bai's mother was washing clothes in the river of Manpo located in Qinglian town, Jiangyou. Suddenly, a fish jumped into her basket, then she cooked and ate it. Soon she got pregnant and finally gave birth to Li Bai".

The legend about the birth of Li Bai is as follows:

The Great White Planet Venus was punished by Jade Emperor to the mortal world. When the Great White Planet Venus went out from the Heavenly Southern Gate and came to Qinglian town, he was impressed by the beautiful landscape, luxuriant vegetation, and rich land there. This place looked like a paradise on earth that was most suitable for living, so he decided to incarnate himself upon it. One day, seeing a dignified and delicate woman washing clothes, he transformed into a golden fish. The golden fish swam towards the riverbank and immediately jumped into her bamboo basket. It had not been very long since she and her husband came here. Seeing a golden fish in her basket, the woman, who was the mother of Li Bai, was so surprised and pleased that she cooked and ate it with her husband that evening. Later, she felt she might be pregnant. One day, Li Bai's mother had a strange dream. She dreamed about the beautiful starry sky and she was attracted by one particular shining star. The brightest star was the Morning Star, also called Venus, which was the first star rising from the western horizon on autumn evenings. It was much brighter than other stars, so Li Bai's mother also admired its beauty. Surprisingly, the star suddenly dropped in Li Bai's mother's arm and immediately she felt a pain in her stomach and afterwards she gave birth to a baby. Due to the dream about the white star, Li Bai's parents decided to name their child Li Bai, and used Tai Bai as his stylistic name. In fact, Li Bai really had a bit of fairy spirit in his adulthood.

2 洁白李花与李白名字由来的故事

春天，百花盛开，姹紫嫣红，春天花木中，第一花当属李花。李花，即李树的花。一树一树绽放的白色花中以李花最引人注目，因为一团一团白色的小花瓣像一个个小雪球挂在树枝上，每一花瓣都如细腻的脂玉，花瓣最外面那层桃红色十分明显，花蕊中开满了许许多多的蕊茎，蕊茎上都长着一个个金灿灿的小圆珠衬托出丰盈，满树的李花就如闪烁的月色。因这样的瓣与蕊，李花就比桃杏要端庄。李花虽花朵较小，但花开繁茂，素雅清新。我国栽培李花也很早，在唐朝时即已普遍。相传白色的李花跟李白名字的由来有个有趣的传说故事呢！

唐代大诗人李白是大家都知道的诗仙。在他出生时，父母为给他起名字煞费苦心，仍不得结果。李白的父亲李客想了个办法："干脆等儿子周岁时，看看他的志向，再考虑一个得体的名字吧。"在李白周岁那年，李白的父亲母亲在桌子上放了许多东西，放了尺子、算盘，以及《尚书》《诗经》等书。李白的母亲抱了他来"抓周"，只见李白看了看，就抓了那本《诗经》。他父亲高兴极了，心想如果儿子长大成了有名的诗人，若没有一个叫得响的好名字岂不遗憾？但思来想去仍不知用什么名字为好，一拖多年没有定名。到李白快7岁该念书上学了，家人这才急了。

这年春天李花盛开，李白一家在青莲陇西院中游玩观赏，在这个还有点微凉的初春，房前屋后李花绚烂，朵朵纯净，朵朵洁白，那迷醉的姿态，还有那诱人的芳香，随一阵清风轻轻扬扬。还在老远，就有一股暗香扑面而来，清新淡雅，不着痕迹。

漫步在李花开满的院子里，李白父亲想写一首春日的七言律诗，有意考考儿子作诗的才能，李白父亲先吟出两句："春风送暖百花开，迎春绽金它先来。"随后说道："后面的诗句我想不出来了，由你们母子二人续下两句吧。"李白的母亲想了一会说："火烧杏林红霞落。"她的话音刚落，李白不假思索地就用手指门外满树白色的李花，脱口说道："李花怒放一树白。"李白父亲听后特别高兴，认为儿子续得绝妙，连声叫好，他越念心里越喜欢，念着念着，他忽然心里一动：这句诗的头一个字不正是自家的姓吗？这最后一个"白"字不正说出了李花圣洁高雅吗？这个字选作孩子的名字真是恰到好处。于是，他当即决定儿子的名字就叫李白。

2 White Plum Flowers and the Origin of Li Bai's Name

In spring, flowers bloom in a blaze of bright colours, but the most striking example must be the plum flower, for the little white petals look like exquisite jades. They look a lot like small snow balls decorated in the trees. One striking feature is the pink surface of the petals. The middle of the flower is full of stems with small golden balls. The plum flowers are like the bright moonlight under these golden balls. Because of these special petals and stems, plum flowers look more elegant than peach blossoms and apricot flowers. Although plum flowers are small, they are lush, elegant and fresh. In China, the cultivation of plum trees has a long history, and it became popular in the Tang Dynasty. There is an interesting legend story about the white plum flowers and Li Bai's name.

Li Bai is widely known as the greatest immortal poet. When he was born, his parents took great pains in choosing a name for him. One day, an idea occurred to Li Bai's father, Li Ke: "On the child's first birthday, we can choose a suitable name for him according to his ambition." There is a traditional Asian custom called "object-grabbing test" on a baby's first birthday occasion to predict its future. On Li Bai's first birthday, his parents put a number of things on the desk including a ruler, an abacus, *Shang Shu*, *Shi Jing* and other books for him to grab. Li Bai looked around, and finally chose *Shi Jing*. His father was very pleased and thought his son would become a famous poet in the future. If so, a good name was very important. But he yet did not know what name was suitable for his son. Li Bai's parents had been very anxious about this until he was 7 years old.

Early in the spring of that year, cool wind woke up the sleeping beauty—the plum flowers. Li Bai and his family had a stroll in their Longxi Garden, which was embraced by heavily perfumed white and elegant plum flowers. The sweet scent of plum flowers met them from far in a quiet, unobtrusive manner.

Walking in a courtyard full of plum flowers, Li Bai's father wanted to make a piece of seven-character verse about spring, and at the same time tested his son's talent in poetry. So Li Bai's father chanted the first two lines: "Flowers are blooming in warm spring breeze, winter jasmines first burst into golden blooms." Then he said: "I'm unable to finish the last two lines, you two continue to finish them please." After thinking for a while, Li Bai's mother continued: "In the sunset fire rosy apricot trees." Just then, Li Bai pointed to the white plum flowers and said without thinking: "Plum trees are blooming with white blossoms." Li Bai's father was very satisfied with his son's answer, and praised him. Repeating this line again and again, suddenly he got an idea and said: "The first word of this line (Li in Chinese version) is just our family name, and the last word 'white' (Bai in Chinese version) implies 'holy' and 'elegant' (the quality of plum flowers). Why don't we name our son according to this?" So he decided to name his son Li Bai.

3 "铁杵磨针"启蒙少年李白的故事

李白从小就是一个非常聪明的孩子，少年时读书很杂，几乎什么书都喜欢看，他从甲乙丙丁、子丑寅卯的汉字开始，认真研读了《论语》《孟子》《老子》《庄子》等诸子百家的书籍，甚至是一些用来推算生辰年月的六十甲子（道家数术历算）方面的书，他也照样看得津津有味。还在他5岁的时候，小小李白就坐在窗前开始摇头晃脑地大声背诵前人有名的文章了。只要两三遍，他就可以毫不费力地把书上的内容背得滚瓜烂熟。后来李白对自己少年时的经历也是津津乐道："五岁诵六甲，十岁观百家"，"十五观奇书，作赋凌相如"。

不过，其实李白当时也是一个贪玩的小孩子，和其他小朋友一样，身上难免有一些缺点，也常常逃学，到乡街上去闲逛。由于李白总是把功课做得很好，所以老师非常喜欢李白，经常在小朋友们面前夸奖他。可是，有一天，老师还在讲课呢，他却听着听着就走神了，一双大眼睛盯着窗外，脑子里竟然想起了昨天晚上妈妈给他讲的金色鲤鱼的故事。李白想："那些小鱼穿着金色的鳞片衣服，在阳光的照耀下闪闪发光，真是太好看了。可是，它们的美丽会不会引来坏人呢？要是被人抓住了，就不能自由自在地游泳了呀，多可怜。"瞧，李白开始陷入他自己编织的幻想的世界里。老师看见李白愣愣的模样，知道他没有认真听课，就停下课来，很生气地说："李白，你站起来重复一遍我刚才讲的话。"李白一下子清醒了，慌忙站起来，却一句话也说不出。"同学们都在笑话我吧！"李白的脸唰地红了，他感到难为情极了。

放学回家的路上，李白还在生自己的气呢。忽然，他发现青莲天宝山下陇西院附近一条清澈的小溪边，一位白发苍苍的老婆婆正在磨一根很粗的铁杵。老婆婆磨得很认真很卖力，大滴大滴的汗珠从老婆婆的额头上滚下来，可是老婆婆只是抬起手用衣袖擦了擦汗，又接着继续磨那根大铁杵了。李白看见老婆婆这么辛苦地磨铁杵，觉得非常好奇。于是他跑上前去，来到老婆婆的身旁，一边轻轻地拉着老婆婆的衣角，一边很有礼貌地说："婆婆，您好。请问您磨这根大铁杵干什么呢？"老婆婆继续专心地磨着她的铁杵，头也不回地说："我呀，我要把它磨成一支细细的绣花针哩。"李白瞪大了眼睛，嘟着嘴说："这么粗的铁杵能磨成针吗？"老婆婆转头看了看李白，见他一脸不相信的样子，这才停下手中的活，蹲下身来，慈祥地对李白说："好孩子，只要功夫深，铁杵也能磨成绣花针哩！"聪明的李白听后深受感动，吃惊之余他像是突然明白了一个深奥的道理，使劲地点了点头，想到自己不认真读书，心中非常惭愧。于是他撒腿便往家跑，重新回到书房，翻开原来读不懂的书，认真读起来。

这件事给李白以深刻的励志教育，他知道了学习应该要有"铁杵磨针"的韧劲，而不能"三天打鱼，两天晒网"，这件事对他以后的学习和生活产生了积极的影响。后来凡是读书碰到困难，他就自然而然地想起"只要功夫深，铁杵磨成针"的教导，从此他便抖擞精神，鼓起勇气，发奋愤读书，果然学问大进。

甚至有一段时间，为了专心读书，他搬到江油大匡山的道观中日夜攻读，每晚都要高挑明灯，一直读到天亮。从此这座山每到夜晚周围几十里都能看得到山尖的灯光，所以人们把这座山叫"点灯山"。李白学成以后，离开故乡，遍游天下，后得唐玄宗召见，很受赏识，封为翰林，于是人们便把李白读书的点灯山叫作"翰林山"。李白在此度过了10年苦读生涯，杜甫诗"匡山读书处，头白好归来"就是指此。因李白在此苦读过书，所以后人就把这里叫作"李白读书台"。

千百年来，无数的文人墨客来这里凭吊李白，而最早一位来这里凭吊李白的，是唐末五代时期的文人杜光庭。为此，杜光庭凭吊李白读书台时留诗一首：

"山中犹有读书台，风扫晴岚画障开。

华月冰壶依然在，青莲居士几时来。"

正是少年李白凭着这种坚持不懈、奋力拼搏的精神，他阅读了大量的书籍，奠定了其学识深度，为他以后取得在诗歌创作上的成功打下了坚实的基础，李白后来终于成了一位了不起的大诗人。

3 The Story of "Grinding an Iron Rod into a Needle" and Young Li Bai

Young Li Bai was very smart and was keen to read various books at hand from the simple Chinese characters "jia yi bing ding" and "zi chou yin mao" to hundreds of various school books that include *The Analects of Confucius*, *Mengzi*,

Laozi and *Zhuangzi,* etc. He read books very carefully with great pleasure, even some books about the cycle of 60 years (Taoist culture) that can be used to calculate dates of birth. When Li Bai was just five years old, he began to read some famous articles aloud by wagging his head. He could memorise the content of a book thoroughly and recite it fluently after reading for two or three times. Later, Li Bai was also very proud of the experiences of his youth and took delight in talking about them: "At five, I could read the classics of Taoism. At ten, I could tell the main thoughts of various schools of Masters." "At fifteen, I began to read some masterpieces, and write poems which could be compared with those of the great Ode Master Sima Xiangru in the Han Dynasty."

But like other kids, young Li Bai was naughty and had some bad manners. He often played truant and used to hang about on the street. However, teachers liked him very much and often praised him in front of other children for his excellent homework. One day, in class, he was absent-minded and gazed out the window. He remembered the story told by his mother the night before about golden fish, thinking: "Those fish with golden clothes that glittered in the sun were really beautiful, but will their beautiful appearance attract the attention of bad people? If they were caught by those bad people, they would not swim freely, how poor they are!" It was clear that Li Bai got absorbed in his own world of fantasy. Seeing Li Bai's silly appearance, his teacher knew that he hadn't listened carefully and as a result, got very angry and stopped the lecture. He asked Li Bai to repeat what he had just said, Li Bai suddenly came to his senses and quickly stood up, but was unable to utter a word. He flushed with embarrassment and was ashamed of his performance, thinking that his classmates must be laughing at him.

Li Bai still was mad at himself after school. Suddenly, he saw a grey-haired old lady sitting by a stream near the Longxi Garden at the foot of Mount Tianbao in Qinglian town, who was exerting herself grinding a big iron bar. The old lady was very serious and large drops of sweat ran down from her forehead, but she just wiped it with her sleeves and continued her work. Driven by curiosity, Li Bai came up, dragging the old lady's clothes and asked her in a polite way: "What are you doing with the iron rod, granny?" "I'm making a sewing needle." said the old lady without stopping grinding. "What?" little Li Bai was puzzled: "You want to grind such thick a rod into a needle?" The old lady turned around, looked at Li Bai, stopped her work and said gently: "Good boy, this doesn't matter. As long as you persevere in doing so, there is nothing you cannot achieve in the world. Of course I can make a needle from the rod." Deeply moved by what the old lady said, Li Bai nodded to agree with her and understood a profound truth. Then he was very ashamed of what he had done in class, so he rushed home and started to read books again in his study.

This incident taught Li Bai an important lesson in both his study and life. He understood that he should not "go fishing for three days and dry the nets for two". He needed tenacious spirit and perseverance in his study. Afterwards, when he had some difficulties with his studies, he would often remember the instruction that "So long as you work hard enough, you can grind an iron rod into a needle—perseverance spells success". From then on, he pulled himself together to study and finally made great progress.

At one time, in order to concentrate on reading, he even moved to a Taoist temple located in the Mount Dakuang, Jiangyou. He studied day and night and burned the midnight oil every night. The residents who lived around the mountain could all see the light on the top of the mountain, so they called this mountain "Light Mountain". After completing his studies there, Li Bai left his homeland and began to travel. Later, he was summoned to serve Emperor Xuanzong who highly respected his work and appointed him as Hanlin (member of the Imperial Academy). So the "Light Mountain" where Li Bai read books was also called "Hanlin Mountain". Afterwards, Li Bai spent 10 years there studying diligently, which can be verified by the verse of Du Fu: "Mount Dakuang was such a good reading place for Li Bai that he stayed there until he was white-haired." It is because Li Bai once read books there that later generations call it the "Reading Platform".

For thousands of years, numerous scholars have been there to pay their respects to him, but Du Guangting, one scholar of the end of the Tang and Five Dynasties, is thought to be the first one. He wrote the following poem in honour of Li Bai:

"The Reading Platform is still in the mountain,
Appearing again after the wind.
The bright moon is shining on the flagon,
But when will Li Bai return?"

It was because of his persistence that Li Bai read a great number of books, which enriched his knowledge and laid a solid foundation for his creation of poetry. Finally, he became a great poet.

4 李白初露头角吟诗惊四座的故事

李白幼年时记忆力特别好。诸子百家，佛经道书，无不过目成诵。据说他5岁就会诵写"六甲"（一种诗体），10岁能读诸子百家的书，懂得了不少天文、地理、历史、文学等各方面的知识。此外，他还学会了弹琴、唱歌、舞蹈、剑术。

相传，李白少年时代，曾经做过一个奇特的梦。一大晚上，李白读书作文之后，酣然入梦。梦中，他仍然在奋笔疾书。突然，他发现自己的笔头上开出一朵洁白如玉的莲花来，光彩夺目，正在诧异之间，一张张白纸又从天而至，落到他的眼前。李白高兴极了，猜想一定是神仙送妙笔给他。想到这里，李白抓起妙笔飞快地写了起来，没想到落在纸上的却是一朵朵盛开的莲花。于是，李白捧起一堆莲花，向青莲陇西院屋外的池塘跑去。他在池边站定，扬手把莲花撒向池水中。顷刻间，奇迹出现了：只见莲花入水后，即刻生出茎叶，竞相绽放。微风吹来，花儿轻轻摇曳，阵阵清香沁人心脾，李白十分欢喜，刚要伸手去摸，忽然醒了过来。李白回忆着梦中的历历情节，十分感慨：这是一个多么神奇美好的梦啊！

说也奇怪，打这之后，李白的才思真就更加敏捷，读书也更加刻苦。这时的少年李白，意气风发，饱读诗书，才华横溢，出口成章，洋溢着同龄孩子少有的儒雅之风和豪放之气。李白不到10岁时，他的名声就传遍了家乡。一次，少年李白随父亲到绵州越王楼赴晚宴，客人们听说李白年少学厚，善于吟诗作赋，想考考他，要他以越王楼为题作诗助兴，李白不慌不忙地站起来，高声吟咏：

"危楼高百尺，手可摘星辰。

不敢高声语，恐惊天上人。"

少年李白借助大胆想象，渲染越王楼之奇高，把越王楼的高耸和夜晚的恐惧写得很逼真，将一座几乎不可想象的宏伟建筑展现在客人面前。吟罢，众人拍手叫好，想不到李白文思如此敏捷，但也有客人怀疑李白去过越王楼，可能是事先写好了的，不如命题作诗，才能考出真本事。于是指着窗外飞舞的一群萤火虫，要李白吟诗一首。李白稍加思索地吟道：

"雨打灯难灭，风吹色更明。

若飞天上去，定作月边星。"

诗的大意是：萤火虫像一盏小灯，雨水打不灭它，风吹过来，它更加明亮，如果飞上天空去，一定能在月亮边当一颗小星。前两句是实写，后两句是想象，虚实结合，表现了萤火虫的美丽形象。少年李白这两首诗作质朴清新，语言浅直，自然天真，想象之大胆奇特让四座皆惊，喝彩声四起，众人一致称赞李白今后一定会成为了不起的人才。

有一年，青莲乡五家坡村民们的小麦总是在晚上被牛吃了，大家互相猜疑，村民们便互相谩骂，可就是没有人站出来承认。被骂的人不服了，便顺着牛蹄印勘察，这一勘察，让人们大惊失色——原来是一头石牛作怪！这头石牛每到夜晚就到处乱跑，践踏庄稼，即使五花大绑也无济于事，村民们束手无策，不知如何是好。少年李白知道此事，便写下了咏石牛的诗句：

"此石巍巍活像牛，埋藏是地数千秋。

风吹遍体无毛动，雨打浑身似汗流。

芳草齐眉难入口，牧童扳角不回头。

自来鼻上无绳索，天地为栏夜不收。"

此诗刻在碑上，立在石牛旁，镇住了石牛。从此这石牛一直静卧不动，不再危害庄稼。现在，这头历经千年风雨的石牛，保存于江油李白纪念馆。据文物专家鉴定，确实是唐宋雕塑风格，为国家一级文物。

后来，人们就将梦笔生花看作是有文才的吉兆，而成语"梦笔生花"就用来形容一个人的才情横溢，文思敏捷。

4. Li Bai Shocks Audience with His Shining Poetic Talents

Li Bai stood out from his peers for his excellent memory. He could recite traditional classics of different schools and religions at his early age. It is said that he could read and write "Liu Jia" (a form of poetry) when he was 5 years old, and he could read books of hundred schools of thought at 10. Therefore, he accumulated considerable knowledge in these fields including astronomy, geography, history and literature, and so forth. In addition, he was also good at playing *guqin*, singing, dancing and practicing swordsmanship.

A legend holds that Li Bai once had a strange dream during his boyhood. In his dream he still worked very hard at his writing, although he was soundly asleep. All of a sudden, he found a jade-white lotus flower blooming on the tip of his writing brush, shining and dazzling. To his surprise, pieces of blank paper drifted down before him. He was so delighted and speculated that it must be a magic writing brush for him sent by God. Thinking of this, he swiftly grasped the magic brush and started to write. Unexpectedly, what he drew on the paper turned out to be blooming lotus flowers. Then, he held a pile of lotuses and ran towards the pond outside Longxi Garden in Qinglian, his hometown, and spread them across the pond. Instantly, a miracle occurred: stems and leaves immediately grew out of those lotuses, and all were in full bloom. The flowers swayed in a gentle, sweet-smelling breeze. Li Bai was so excited that he stretched out his hand to touch them when he suddenly awoke. He started to recall the details of his dream and thought aloud with a long sigh: what a miraculous and beautiful dream!

Oddly enough, from then on, Li Bai had a quicker mind and studied harder than ever before. Young Li Bai, who was high-spirited and vigorous, well-read and learned, brilliant and eloquent, bold and unconstrained, was well-known in his hometown. One day, he attended a banquet in Yuewang Tower with his father. Guests wanted to test his chanting ability and verify his fame. They asked him to create a poem about Yuewang Tower. At guests' request, Li Bai stood up calmly and chanted aloud:

"Hundred feet high the Summit Temple stands,
Where I could pluck the stars with my own hands.
At dead of night I dare not speak aloud,
For fear of waking dwellers in the cloud."

(From *The Selected Poems of Li Bai* by Xu Yuanchong)

Young Li Bai rendered Yuewang Tower as a very high building using his bold imagination. He depicted vividly the height of Yuewang Tower and the horror of the evening, presenting a magnificent building which was beyond people's imagination. After hearing Li Bai's chanting, guests applauded and were surprised by his quick mind and wit. However, there were a few guests who suspected he had visited Yuewang Tower before and had made a poem in advance. Therefore, they suggested that he compose another poem using a certain topic assigned to test a his real talent. They pointed to a swarm of glowworms flying outside a window and asked him to make a poem. After thinking for a while, Li Bai chanted:

"Harder to put out your fine when the rain beats,
But brighter when the wind blows.
If you go into the sky,
You will be a moon star."

The brief meaning of this poem is: a glowworm is like a little lamp which could not be extinguished by rain. Instead, it becomes brighter as the wind blows. Flying into the sky, it would be a star near the moon. The first two lines were based on reality and the last two lines on imagination, shaping a beautiful image of a glowworm. The two poems chanted by young Li Bai are in plain and straight-forward language, giving a sense of naivety and natural speech. His bold imagination and the visionary picture showed in the poem won cheers and applause for him. All witnesses believed that he was bound to be a great talent.

One year, villagers in Wujiapo, Qinlian township, frequently found their wheat seedlings eaten by buffalo in the evening. They began to suspect each other and started to abuse each other. However, nobody confessed. Those people who were abused felt aggrieved, so they began to seek clues following the buffalo's hoofprints. And the final result stunned all people—it turned out to be a stone buffalo. The buffalo would run about wildly when night fell, treading on crops, even when it was tied up. The villagers did not know how to deal with it. Hearing this story, Li Bai wrote this poem in praise of the stone buffalo:

"As lofty as an ox, for thousands of years the stone buried under the ground.

No hair moving in winds, but sweat dripping in rains.

No access to the grass, or no return of head with the pull of horn by the shepherd.

No rope on the nose, or no chain on the fence with heaven and earth as the stable."

The poem was inscribed on a stone tablet which was set up beside the stone buffalo to pacify it. Hence, the stone buffalo laid there quietly, doing no harm to crops. Now, the stone buffalo, who witnessed thousands of years of twists and turns, was preserved in the Memorial Hall of Li Bai in Jiangyou, Western China. According to experts of cultural relics, it was a national first-class relic, in a sculptural style of the Tang and Song Dynasty.

Afterwards, people regarded "flowers appearing on writing brushes in one's dream" as a fortune of great talents, and this idiom was often used to describe a person with great talent and intelligence.

5 李白续诗辛辣讽刺县令的故事

唐代大文学家李白少年时期，曾一度贪图玩耍，不爱学习。有一次，他偶然看到一位老婆婆在用铁杵磨针，深受启发。从此发奋学习，学业大进，闻名乡里。后来，经乡里文人举荐，16岁的李白到彰明县衙门里当了一名文书小吏，经常出入县衙内。

一次，少年李白牵牛从县令大堂下的敞厅经过，也许这天正好赶上县令夫人心情不爽，也许李白的经过打扰了她的美梦，总之，当时县令夫人看到李白牵着一头老黄牛，竟然从堂下敞厅大摇大摆地走过，一股无名之火涌上心头，气势汹汹地吼道："牛都牵进县衙里来了！谁家的黄毛娃儿，竟然如此不懂规矩，乡镇上大路条条，你走哪条不行，却偏偏从老娘这里经过，这还成何体统！"骂完以后，又要县令惩治少年李白。

李白见县令夫人如此胡搅蛮缠，有心捉弄她一番，于是，眉头一皱，计上心来。只见李白抬头看了看县令夫人，不慌不忙地走上前去，向县令夫人赔礼道歉，并随口吟诗一首：

"素面倚栏钩，娇声出外头。

若非是织女，何必问牵牛？"

县令夫人本来就对什么诗词音律一窍不通，见这个放牛娃儿竟然信口吟诵出一首诗来，大为惊讶，于是，对少年李白的才思敏捷十分佩服，便饶过了他。其实，她哪里知道，少年李白在这首诗中巧妙地将自己比作神话传说中的牛郎，以县令之妻并不是神话传说中的织女为由，认为她不应该责罚自己牵牛从堂下经过。这首诗既切合当时的形势和自己的身份，又不露形迹，隐晦含蓄而又明白易晓。故县令听后也感到十分惊奇，并未责问此事。

不久，春耕开始，县令要下乡视察，少年李白随身伺候。黄昏时走到紫云山下，碰到农民放火烧荒。县令看到山上烈火熊熊燃烧，诗兴大发，拖长声音吟道："野火烧山后，人归火不归。"吟了这两句再也吟不出来了，急得满头大汗。这时李白从容地吟道：

"焰随红日远，烟逐暮云飞。"

这两句不仅对仗工整，文字精练，而且写景生动形象，将山火蔓延之势与傍晚日光彩霞融为一体。李白这两句诗一出口，顿使县令羞愧难言，再不敢往下吟了。

转眼夏天来到。一日绵州涪江涨大水，淹没了大片良田，冲毁了许多民房。可昏庸的彰明县令不但不设法救灾，反而硬拉着衙门里的人去观赏水景。

他们来到江边，只见黄水滔滔，急流似箭，浊浪中，卷杂着破板烂席、残枝败叶。忽然，有人惊叫起来："死人！"众人随他手指方向仔细一瞧，果然有一具女尸从上游漂下，猛地一个大浪，尸体被冲到岸边，在芦苇丛中转了几转，一会儿又不见了。

面对被溺死的女子，脑满肠肥的县令却诗兴大发，摇头晃脑地吟唱起来："二八谁家女，漂来倚岸芦。鸟窥眉上翠，鱼弄口旁珠。"只吟出这几句，他就吭吭哧哧接不下去了。

被迫随行的李白早就心中有气，眼下看到昏庸的县令竟以死尸寻欢作乐，更是火顶脑门，于是满怀疾愤之情，续了四句：

"绿发随波散，红颜逐浪无。

因何逢伍相？应是怨秋胡。"

这首诗的后两句用了两个典故。

"伍相"即春秋时期的伍子胥。当年他被楚兵追杀，蒙一位浣纱女相救，伍子胥很感激她，但又怕浣纱女向楚兵告密，于是犹豫不定。浣纱女为了让他快逃，只能投水自杀以表清白。多年以后，李白写了一篇《溧阳濑水贞义女碑铭》，歌颂的正是这位浣纱女。

"秋胡"是春秋时期鲁国人，他婚后第五天就被派到外地当官去了。五年后回来，见到路旁有一位美女在采桑。秋胡就拿出金子来想调戏她，被这个女子严词拒绝了。秋胡又四处逛了逛，然后回到家里，母亲把他妻子喊了出来，秋胡一看就傻眼了，原来自己妻子正是那个采桑女。秋胡的妻子是位烈性女子，见自己日思夜想的丈夫居然是这种人，悲愤不已，就投河而死。

诗中，李白辛辣地讽刺县令就像春秋时期行为不轨、玩弄妇女的秋胡，应该让被吴王夫差冤杀的伍子胥化作怒潮淹死。县令一听，脸色顿变，半天说不出一句话来。李白料定县令必将寻机报复，便收拾行装，弃职回家了。

后来，不知怎么的，这些故事就在当地传播开来，人们都知道了少年李白作诗嘲弄彰明县令和夫人的事，对李白的才学和胆识十分佩服。

5 Li Bai Satirizes the County Magistrate with Poems

Li Bai, the great litterateur of the Tang Dynasty, was a playful boy with no interest in studying during his boyhood. Once, he saw an elderly lady sharpening a needle from an iron bar. Deeply inspired by that lady, he determined to study hard and later he was rewarded for his endeavour when his name spread across the whole county. Later, after being recommended by scholars in his county, 16-year-old Li Bai acted as an amanuensis in *yamen* (government office in imperial China) in Zhangming County, which gave him opportunities to contact the county magistrate.

Once, young Li Bai, leading a buffalo, went through the widely-opened magistrate lobby hall, which infuriated the magistrate's wife, who perhaps happened to be in a bad mood, or perhaps was interrupted in her sweet dream by Li Bai's by-passing, so she yelled at Li Bai: "How dare you take a buffalo here? Where is this ignorant boy from? Do you know the rules? There are so many roads in the county, and why did you choose to pass through here? How unreasonable it is!"

Still angry, she urged her husband, the magistrate, to punish young Li Bai.

After observing the magistrate's wife acting so rudely and unreasonably, Li Bai decided to play a trick on her. He thought for a moment and an idea came to his mind. He raised his head and looked at the magistrate's wife, and apologized to her. Then, without thinking, he chanted:

"Leaning against handrails with no make-up, and sweet voice can be heard faraway.

If you were not a weaving girl, why should you still ask a cowherd boy?"

Knowing nothing about poetry at all, the magistrate's wife was extremely surprised at this cowherd boy who could chant a poem at ease. Therefore, she decided to forgive him out of admiration for his quick wits. In fact, she didn't know that young Li Bai skilfully compared himself to the Cowherd in a fairy tale, and made an excuse for saying that the magistrate's wife was not the Weaving Girl (The Cowherd and the Weaving Girl are from an old Chinese fairy tale), implying that she should not punish him for his former behaviour. This poem not only fit with the situation and Li Bai's status at that time, but also satirized the magistrate's wife. Hearing this, the county magistrate was also deeply surprised, so he did not blame Li Bai.

Soon, spring ploughing started and the county magistrate inspected the countryside with Li Bai serving around. At dusk, they walked to the foot of Mount Ziyun and came across farmers setting fire to grass on the waste land. Seeing the blazing fire on the mountain, the county magistrate felt a strong urge to make a poem, so he chanted: "A mountain was burnt by wild fire, and people backed home but fire never backed." Finishing these two lines, he couldn't continue anymore, so he felt embarrassed with sweat dripping from his forehead. At this time, Li Bai chanted at ease:

"Flames went far away with the glowing sun, and smoke flied with evening clouds."

These two lines were not only well-paralleled in structure, concise in words, but also depicted the scenery vividly, skilfully merging the pervading mountain fire with rosy clouds at dusk. After hearing Li Bai's two lines, the county magistrate was too shamed to utter any words and did not dare to chant anymore.

In a twinkling, summer came. One day, the Fujiang River in Mianzhou flooded, destroying many residences. However, that fatuous county magistrate forced his staff in *yamen* to watch the flood water instead of trying to help save lives.

They came to the riverside only to find a surge of flood water. All of a sudden, someone screamed: "A dead body!" Looking in the direction he pointed to, the crowd really saw a female corpse drifting along the riverside.

Facing the drowned lady, the county magistrate — a fat idiot — was eager to make a poem and chanted: "Where is the young lady from? Drifted here and leaned on reeds offshore. Birds peeked at her eyebrow, and fish played on her lips." After making these lines, he started to hum and haw and could not continue.

Forced to follow the county magistrate closely, Li Bai was frustrated and angry. Seeing the fatuous county magistrate making fun of a dead body, he could not control his anger anymore, so he continued to chant the next four lines:

"Green hair dispersed with waves,
And a beauty chased waves around.
Why did she meet prime minister Wu?
Probably she complained Qiuhu."

The latter two lines of this poem quoted two literary allusions.

"prime minister Wu" is Wu Zixu lived in Chunqiu period. In those days, he was chased by Chu troops but was saved by a lady washing gauzes nearby. Wu deeply appreciated her help, but also feared that she would reveal his tracks to Chu troops, so he hesitated and did not know whether to go or not. In order to let Wu escape as quickly as possible, the gauze-washing lady committed suicide by jumping into water to show her innocence. Many years later, Li Bai wrote an article *Epitaph of the Courageous Girl alongside Lai River in Liyang*, which praised the gauze-washing lady who saved Wu Zixu's life. This story was quite popular among people.

"Qiu Hu" was from the Lu State during Chunqiu period and he was assigned to other places acting as an official only five days after his marriage. Five years later, on his way back home he found a beautiful lady harvesting mulberry leaves at a roadside. Then he tried to impress and flirt with the girl, but she flatly rejected him. After he strolled back home, his mother called his wife to come out to meet him. To Qiu Hu's great surprise, his wife turned out to be the girl picking mulberry leaves. After Qiu Hu's wife realised she had rejected her husband after longing for so many years, she committed suicide by drowning herself.

In the poem, Li Bai tartly satirized the county magistrate by depicting him as Qiu Hu who misbehaved and liked womanising during Chunqiu period and he thought that Qiu should be drowned by the raging tides which were transformed by Wu Zixu, who was wrongly killed by King Fuchai of Wu State. After hearing Li Bai's poem, the county magistrate's face scowled instantly and he could not say a word for a long time. Predicting that the county magistrate would take revenge, Li Bai packed up, resigned and went home.

These stories were later spread among the locals, and everyone knew and admired Li Bai—the boy who had mocked the county magistrate and his wife.

6 李白漫游蜀中驯养禽鸟的故事

中国古代文人的漫游是我国传统旅游文化的一个重要方面。他们大都把漫游看成是超凡脱俗、完善人格，或是求知寻美，对社会生活所造成的生理、心理失衡的一种暂时补偿手段，而加以推崇和追求。漫游成为当时文人的一种存在方式。他们遍游名山大川，并以此为题材写出许多举世瞩目的传世之作。

20岁左右，李白在四川家乡的匡山读书，师从纵横家赵蕤学习纵横术。李白勤奋好学，"常横经籍书，制作不倦"。在20岁以后，李白游历了蜀中不少名胜古迹。蜀中雄伟壮丽的山川，培育了李白开阔的襟怀、豪放的性格和对大自然的热爱。受纵横家和儒家思想的影响，李白有着很强的事业心，希望建功立业；但他又受道教和道家思想影响较深，热切地向往着求仙学道的隐逸生活。这种矛盾的生活理想，在他身上最后形成二者兼顾的愿望，即"功成，名遂，身退"。

在李白15～25岁的十年间，李白主要在蜀中漫游。四川昌隆所在的绵州地区，自汉末以来，便是道教活跃的地方。因此，李白从少年时起，常去戴天山寻找道观的道士谈论道经。李白少年时代的诗歌留下来不多，比较早的一篇是《访戴天山道士不遇》。说的是有一天李白到深山的道观中去寻访一位道士。时值初春季节，桃花正带露开放，飞瀑流泉，野竹小鹿，山中景色确实美不胜收。然而道士却始终没有回来，从早晨到下午，一直见不到人影，他只好悻悻而归了。回到家后愈想愈觉得那道士真是如同不食人间烟火的神人，他再也按捺不住诗兴，于是展纸挥笔：

"犬吠水声中，桃花带露浓。

树深时见鹿，溪午不闻钟。

野竹分青霭，飞泉挂碧峰。

无人知所去，愁倚两三松。"

李白出生并成长在蜀中家乡这如诗如画、雄奇秀美的奇山异水之中，在这里生活了整整25年，几乎占了其人生的一半。他能自幼孕育出对美丽山河的浓烈热爱和对大自然强烈的崇尚、向往之情，是丝毫也没有什么奇怪的了。李白精力充沛，对什么都兴致勃勃。他在家乡除了读书和习剑，更多的是访道、隐居和游历，其足迹遍及了家乡的山山水水。对于家乡的奇山异水，李白自己在诗中是这样描绘的：

"石磴层层上太华，白云深处有人家。

道旁对月闲吹笛，仙子乘云运驾车。

怪石堆山如坐虎，老藤缠树似腾蛇。

曾闻玉井今何在，会见蓬莱十丈花。"

这是李白笔下的太华山景观。大匡山与太华山乃同一山脉，紧紧相依，从大匡山大明寺逶迤西北上，走十余里即到太华观。《太华观》就是写他访拜太华观道士的见闻，展示了古朴清幽的山中景色，描写了深山月下、笛声悠扬、仙子乘云的神仙境界。《寻雍尊师隐居》这首诗为李白少年时在四川故乡寻仙访道所作，诗人着力渲染匡山有声有色、有动有静的山水花木、峭壁飞泉，幽美绚丽的景色烘托出淡淡的愁思与怅然：

"群峭碧摩天，逍遥不记年。

拨云寻古道，倚树听流泉。

花暖青牛卧，松高白鹤眠。

语来江色暮，独自下寒烟。"

李白的这段漫游时期，正当唐朝开元盛世，他的许多诗都已充分显示他的艺术才华。李白除了漫游蜀中的名胜古迹外，还与道观的道士仰观天文，俯察地理，求道证道。后来，他与一位号为东严子的隐者隐居于岷山，多年不进城市。隐居期间，他还在自己居住的山林里，饲养了许多奇禽异鸟。据史料记载，大诗人李白还是一位驯养禽鸟的高手呢！

20岁左右时，李白曾一度隐居在四川成都附近的青城山。他在山中除读书、练剑之外，就是精心驯养一大群禽鸟。这些美丽而有灵性的鸟儿，由于被饲养驯化，所以会定时飞来求食。好像能听懂人的语言，一声呼唤，便从四处飞落阶前、人肩上，甚至可以在人的手里啄食谷粒，一点都不害怕。不像宫廷里那些养在笼中的鸟，不解人意，缺乏灵性。李白在他后来所做的《上安州裴长史书》一文中说："昔与逸人东严子隐于岷山之阳，白巢居数年，不迹城市。养奇禽千计。呼皆就掌取食，了无惊猜。广汉太守闻而异之，诣庐亲睹，因举二以有道，并不起。此白养高忘机，不屈之迹也。"可见他饲养的禽鸟不仅数量惊人，而且他能令禽鸟听从他的号令在他的掌中取食，说明他驯养禽鸟的技术是相当高超的。

李白驯鸟这件事被远近传作奇闻，最后传到了广汉太守的耳朵里，于是太守亲自到山中观看鸟儿们的就食情况，想验证一下传闻是否真如那般神奇。当这位太守亲眼看见李白和东严子能指挥鸟类的行动，内心大为惊讶，便认定他们有道术，是功力深厚的道人，当下便想推荐二人去参加道科的考试。可是，此时的李白年少轻狂，不屑以此为进身之阶，而隐者东严子更是淡泊名利无心从政，所以二人都婉言谢绝了太守的盛情。

李白喜养禽鸟终生不倦。即使他在政治上失意，到处漂泊之时，也乐此不疲。李白精心驯养的一大群禽鸟中，最得李白宠爱的鸟是一对有着"鹛类之王"誉称的画眉鸟。同时还有一种深得李白钟爱的鸟是白鹇鸟，又名白雉。这是一种白色的大鸟，样子似鹳似鹤，却又非鹳非鹤。然而此鸟极难驯养，李白后来只得去黄山求鸟。黄山隐士胡公养有一对白鹇，是由家鸡孵化，从小饲养长大的，十分驯服。李白在青城山时曾养过此鸟，但因此鸟野性较强而没有驯养成功。所以他对胡公的白鹇掩饰不住钟爱之情，表示了君子要夺人所好之意。胡公欣然答应奉送双鹇，但要求"谪仙人"亲笔题诗一首，李白欣喜若狂，马上写了《赠黄山胡公求白鹇》五言律诗一首赠之：

"请以双白璧，买君双白鹇。
白鹇白如锦，白雪耻容颜。
照影玉潭里，刷毛琪树间。
夜栖寒月静，朝步落花闲。
我愿得此鸟，玩之坐碧山。
胡公能辍赠，笼寄野人还。"

李白在诗文中透露了他热衷喜养白鹇禽鸟的心情，他在《赠黄山胡公求白鹇》一诗中的前序里向我们道明了此事的缘由和过程："闻黄山胡公有双白鹇，盖是家鸡所伏，自小驯狎，了无惊猜，以其名呼之，皆就掌取食。然此鸟耿介，尤难畜之。予平生酷好，竟莫能致。而胡公辍赠于我，唯求一诗。闻之欣然，适会宿意，援笔三叫，文不加点以赠之。"在诗中李白以白鹇与白璧相提并论，以白锦喻白鹇毛色之美，表达出自己得到珍禽后的欣喜之情。诗中极力赞美白鹇高洁纯美，超脱不凡，以寄托诗人的志趣。同时也写出了诗人与胡公以诗鸟互赠的真挚友情，还寄托了诗人不凡的生活志趣和独特的审美观点。

正是因为李白那一时期的养鸟经历，才让他在今后诗文中有关鸟类的诗句大放异彩。这才让我们今天的后人看到了"众鸟高飞尽，孤云独去闲""人行明镜中，鸟度屏风里""好鸟迎春歌后院，飞花送酒舞前檐""但见悲鸟号古木，雄飞雌从绕林间"等流传千古、脍炙人口的美丽诗句。李白对驯养禽鸟的浓厚兴趣，折射出他热爱生命、崇尚自然的积极的人生观。

6 Li Bai Travels around and Domesticates Birds in Shu

In ancient China, scholars often went traveling to broaden their horizons. Most of them regarded traveling as a way to become an otherworldly person, to boost their personality or to seek knowledge or beauty, and to temporarily compensate physical and psychological imbalance caused by their social lives. Travel became a lifestyle for scholars at that time, so they traveled all over famous mountains and rivers and wrote many handed-down masterpieces based on their travel experiences.

When he was about 20 years old, Li Bai started to learn political strategies from strategist Zhao Rui in Mount Dakuang in his hometown Jiangyou, Sichuan province. He was so diligent and eager for knowledge that he often put books beside his pillow and wrote tirelessly. After 20, Li Bai traveled to quite a few scenic and historic sites in Shu. Magnificent mountains and rivers in Shu nourished his open mind, bold and unconstrained character and love for nature. Influenced by political strategists and Confucianism, he had a strong ambition for career and achievements. But, with more influence from Taoism and Taoists, he also eagerly looked forward to a secluded life pursuing immortality and learning Taoism. These paradoxical life ideals were finally forged into his pursuit of "achievements, reputation and seclusion".

Between the ages of 15 and 25, Li Bai mainly traveled in Shu. Changlong county, Sichuan province, located in Mianzhou area, had been a place where Taoism was active since the end of the Han Dynasty. Therefore, since his boyhood, he often looked for Taoists in temples to discuss Taoism. A few of the poems he wrote during his boyhood witnessed his experience, and one of them was *Calling on Taoist Recluse in Mount Daitian without Meeting Him*. It said: One day Li Bai went to a temple in thick woods to call on the Taoist in an early spring when peach blossoms were tinged with dew, rippling brooks and tumbling cascades ran, wild deer chased in bamboo forests. The sceneries in the mountain were really magnificent. However, after waiting from morning to evening, Li Bai was disappointed to find no Taoist, so he had to turn back. After going back home, he thought that the Taoist was an otherworldly immortal, so he could not constrain himself from writing this poem:

"Dogs' barks are muffled by the rippling brook,
Peach blossoms tinged with dew much redder look.
In the thick woods a deer is seen at times,
Along the stream I hear no noonday chimes.

In the blue haze which wild bamboo divide,
Tumbling cascades hang on green mountain side.
Where is the Taoist gone? None can tell me.
Saddened, I lean on this or that pine tree."

(From *The Selected Poems of Li Bai* by Xu Yuanchong)

Li Bai was born and grew up in Shu—a place of picturesque, magnificent and exotic mountains and waters. He lived there for 25 years, almost half of his whole life. No wonder Li Bai developed an ardent love for beautiful scenery and a strong worship and yearning for nature. He was always vigorous and curious. Apart from reading and practicing sword fighting, his activities covered calling on Taoists, living a secluded life and traveling, marking his footprints on mountains and rivers in his hometown. As for the exotic mountains and waters in his hometown, Li Bai described them in his poem like this:

"Stone steps to Taihua,
Households are seen in thick clouds.
Fluting to the moon alongside the path,
And fairy carrying carriage by clouds.

Jagged rocks pile like tigers,

And vine rolling trees like flying snakes.

Where is the jade well,

Where I can see the Penglai flowers."

The description above was about the scenery of Mount Taihua. Mount Dakuang and Mount Taihua are in the same mountain range, being closely adjacent to each other. Meandering all the way northwest upward from the Daming Temple in the Mount Dakuang, you could come to Taihua Taoist Temple after more than ten *li*'s walk. *Taihua Taoist Temple* was about what he saw and heard there when he called on the Taoist in the Taihua Taoist Temple, presenting simple and quiet sceneries in the mountain and depicting a fairyland in thick woods with the sound of melodious flute and fairy riding clouds in the bright moonlight. Li Bai wrote *Seeking the Seclusion of Taoist Yong* during his travels around Sichuan in his boyhood, rendering vividly and dramatically the waters, mountains, flowers and woods of Mount Dakuang surrounded by sounds, colours, tranquility and movements. This poem also depicted steep cliffs, waterfalls and secluded and splendid landscapes contrasting his gloomy moods and disappointment:

"Steep peaks lead to blue sky,

Living carefree without remembering years.

Pushing aside thick clouds to look for ancient paths,

And listening to pouring waterfalls by leaning against trees.

Among warm flowers lie black cows,

And on high pines sleep white cranes.

Dusk hazes gather on river after long talks,

I have to go down the cold and hazed hill alone."

It happened to be the prosperous Kaiyuan Age of the Tang Dynasty when Li Bai was traveling around, so many of his poems fully reflected his artistic talents.

Apart from traveling to scenic and historic sites in Shu, Li Bai also observed horoscopes, studied geography and sought and testified Taoism. He and a recluse named Dong Yanzi lived in seclusion in Mount Min for many years without going downhill. During the period of seclusion, he raised many exotic birds in the woods where he lived. According to historical records, Li Bai, a great poet, was actually an expert in domesticating birds!

When he was about 20 years old, Li Bai once secluded himself in Mount Qingcheng near Chengdu, Sichuan province. Except reading and practicing sword fighting, he elaborately raised a flock of birds. Being tamed, these beautiful and nimble birds would regularly fly to him for food. They acted as if they could understand what people were saying. Hearing a call, they would fly to steps or on people's shoulders, even on people's hands for grains without any fear. Unlike those birds kept in cages in the royal court, these birds tamed by Li Bai were intelligent enough to understand people's feelings. He later said in *A Letter to General Secretary Pei of Anzhou*: "In the past, I, with a recluse named Dong Yanzi, lived in seclusion in the southern Mount Min, and lived a simple life there without going downhill for many years. We raised thousands of exotic birds. After hearing a calling, they would fly to people's hands for grains without any fear. Hearing this, the Prefecture Chief in Guanghan was very curious and paid a visit to my house and recommended us to take examinations in Taoist arts. However, we all refused him, and the chief praised that I was a noble person with pure interest who never surrendered to the rich and the power and never followed the worldly traditions and affairs." It could be seen that he not only raised numerous birds but also trained his birds to follow his instructions and peck grains out of his hand, which showed he had a very superb skill in taming birds.

Li Bai's bird-taming was spread as a fantastic story by people around, and finally it was spread to the Prefecture Chief of Guanghan. Hence, the Prefecture Chief went to the mountain to watch how those birds were fed to verify whether the story was true. When he saw Li Bai and Dong Yanzi commanding birds, he was very surprised, so he thought they were Taoists who had Taoist magic arts and deep capabilities. Therefore, he wanted to recommend them to take examinations in Taoist arts. However, Li Bai disdained it as a stepping-stone for further development, and the recluse, Dong Yanzi, was even more indifferent to fame and wealth and was not interested in politics, so they two declined the Prefecture Chief's recommendation.

Taming birds was Li Bai's lifelong and tireless hobby. He was never bored with it even when he didn't go well in his political career and wandered here and there. Among those elaborately tamed birds by him, a pair of thrushes, with a fame of "The King of Thrushes", was his favourite. Lophura nycthemera was also cherished by Li Bai. This is a big white bird resembling stork or crane, which was difficult to tame, so Li Bai had to seek birds in Mount Huang later. Recluse Hu raised a pair of silver pheasants there, which were hatched by chicken and fed by humans from an early age, so they were very docile. Li Bai had kept this kind of birds before in Mount Qingcheng, but could not tame them successfully because of their wild nature. So he could not conceal his admiration for the silver pheasants owned by Mr. Hu and declared that he wanted to own Mr. Hu's favourite birds. Mr. Hu readily promised him the birds, but asked for a poem written by the "Demoted Immortal" (Li Bai) in exchange. Being wild with joy, Li Bai wrote a five-character octave for him, named *To Mr. Hu in Mount Huang for the Silver Pheasants*:

"I want to buy your silver pheasants,
Using a pair of white jades.
Their feathers are as white as white brocade,
Making white shameful.
The silver pheasants admire themselves in the jade pool,
And tidy their feathers in grasses and trees.
Taking a rest under the cold moon quietly in the evening,
And going for a walk among fallen petals in the morning.
I wish to have this pair of silver pheasants,

Playing with them among green mountains and blue waters.
If Mr. Hu sent them to me,
I would bring them home in cages."

Li Bai showed his ardent love for raising silver pheasants in his poem and explained why and how he loved those birds in the preface to *To Mr. Hu in Mount Huang for the Silver Pheasants*: "I heard that Mr. Hu in Mount Huang raised a pair of silver pheasants which were hatched by chickens and raised by humans. That may sound unsurprising. If they were called by someone, they would fly to his hand for food. However, these birds were special and particularly difficult to tame. I could not tame them though I am good at this. But, Mr. Hu was willing to give me a pair of silver pheasants in exchange for a just a poem from me. I was so delighted that this was just what I had desired. So I started to write a poem at one stretch without any correction, and sent it to Mr. Hu." In this poem, Li Bai bracketed the silver pheasants and white jade, and compared the white feather of silver pheasants to white brocade, expressing his delight after accepting the rare birds. He highly praised the silver pheasants' noble, beautiful and otherworldly aura to express his own aspirations and interest. Meanwhile, this poem also depicted the sincere friendship between Li Bai and Mr. Hu, who exchanged birds for poems, and showed Li Bai's extraordinary life interests and unique aesthetic view.

His experiences in raising birds in this period appeared in his later poems. So we could read many well-known eternal poems spreading through ages including: "All birds have flown away, so high; A lonely cloud drifts on, so free." "In the mirror bright boats hie; Between the screens birds fly." "Good birds welcome spring by singing in backyard; Falling flowers bring wines and dance before eve." and "Cuckoos are heard crying on old tress, male birds followed by females fly in the forest." Li Bai's keen interest in raising and domesticating birds reflected his positive outlook on life: love for life and worship of nature.

7 李白辞蜀远游的故事

李白的父亲李客没有当过官,是个很有文化修养的大商人,对家里的子弟要求很严。李白是李客第12个儿子,从小聪慧过人,学习又十分刻苦,李客非常疼爱他,而且精心培养他。李白5岁时,李客就指导他诵读汉代著名文学家司马相如的辞赋,并常对他说:"孩子,你要为我们李门争气,希望你将来也成为司马相如那样有成就的人。"李白把父亲的殷切期望铭记在心,立志做一个超过司马相如的文学家。一天,他经过几次修改,把一篇辞赋写好了,便兴冲冲地送给父亲看。他自认为写得不错,一定会得到父亲的夸奖。不料,父亲读了以后,很不满意,对他说:"你这篇赋写得太差了,既无气势,又乏文采。不过你也不要灰心,应当继续努力。"

李白点了点头,说:"一定按照父亲的要求办。"回到书房,他把那份文稿投到火炉中烧了。然后重新构思,重新创作,连续拟作了三次,没有一次感到满意,只得都付之一炬,直到第四次,才写成比较满意的两篇,即《拟别赋》《拟恨赋》。《拟别赋》后来散失了,《拟恨赋》还保留着,收在宋人宋敏求所编的《李太白集》中。

25岁时,李白已经成为一个多才多艺的人。他不仅能诗善文,而且会击剑骑马,还喜欢弹琴唱歌。他决心为国家干一番轰轰烈烈的事业,就对父亲说:"孩儿打算离家到外面去长长见识。""还是在家读读书,有机会找个事做吧,何必远离家乡外出呢?"父亲说。李白满怀豪情地说:"大丈夫活在世上,应该志在四方,胸怀天下。待在家乡怕是没法施展我的才能。出去以后,一来可以游历各地,结交名士;二来也可以寻找机会,辅助皇上。"

父亲听了,乐呵呵地笑着说:"好,你既然有这样的抱负,那就出去闯闯吧!"

过了几天,李白告别父母,身佩宝剑,上路了。李白乘船沿着长江东下,过三峡的时候,江水湍急,船行如箭,他站立船头,望着两岸的青山,心中非常激动。后来他写过好几首描写三峡风光的诗。有一首是:

"朝辞白帝彩云间，千里江陵一日还。

两岸猿声啼不住，轻舟已过万重山。"

在漫游途中，李白还登上庐山，观望瀑布，写下了《望庐山瀑布》二首。其中一首是：

"日照香炉生紫烟，遥看瀑布挂前川。

飞流直下三千尺，疑是银河落九天。"

在李白的诗里，祖国山河多么壮美呀！他的诗自然又流畅，毫不造作，不愧是大诗人的手笔。

7 Li Bai Travels Faraway outside Shu

Li Ke, Li Bai's father and a well-educated businessman, was very strict with his children. Li Bai, the twelfth son in the family, was more intelligent than other children and studied harder, so he was loved very much and fostered carefully by his father. When he was 5 years old, his father guided him to read poems and odes written by Sima Xiangru, the famous litterateur in the Han Dynasty. His father always said to him: "My child, you should work hard for our family Li and I wish you to be a successful man like Sima Xiangru in the future." Bearing his father's wishes in mind, Li Bai resolved to be a litterateur exceeding Sima Xiangru. One day, after several modifications, he finally finished an ode and felt excited to show it to his father. He thought his work was quite good and would be praised by his father. To his surprise, after reading it, his father was dissatisfied with it and said to him: "What you wrote was really awful for lack of vigour and literary grace. However, you should not feel frustrated but should continue to work harder."

Li Bai nodded: "I will work hard as you require." Back to his study, he put that draft into fire and then began to conceive and create a new one. However, after three attempts in succession with no satisfactory results, he put them all into fire. Not until the fourth time did he compose two quite satisfactory odes, which were *Ode of Farewell* and *Ode of Hatred*. The former was lost, but the latter was still kept in *Anthology of Li Bai* compiled by Song Minqiu who lived in the Song Dynasty.

By the age of 25, Li Bai had already become a versatile young man. Not only could he write poems and essays, but he was also a skilled horse-rider and sword fighter and was fond of singing and playing the zither. He determined to make a great contribution to his own country, so he said to his father: "I decided to go out and widen my horizons." His father replied: "Why not study at home and find a job once having an opportunity? Why take the trouble to go far from home?" Full of enthusiasm, he said: "Living in this world, a real man should be ambitious and bear the whole world in his mind. I could not exert my full talents if I stayed in my hometown. If I went out, on the one hand, I could travel to different places and make friends with celebrities; on the other hand, I could help the emperor if I was given a chance."

Hearing this, his father laughed and said: "Ok, now that you have such an ambition, you should go for it!"

A few days later, after bidding farewell to his parents, Li Bai set out with a sword. Moving eastward along the Yangtze River, he saw the river was surging forward with boats lining up like arrows. Standing at the prow and watching mountains along the river banks, he felt extremely excited. Later, he wrote a few poems about the sceneries in the Three Gorges. One of those is:

"Leaving at dawn the White Emperor crowned with cloud,
I've sailed a thousand *li* through Three Gorges in a day.
With monkeys' sad adieux the riverbanks are loud,
My skiff has left ten thousand mountains far away."

On his way of traveling around, Li Bai climbed Mount Lu, watched the waterfall and wrote two poems titled *The Waterfall in Mount Lu Viewed from Afar*. One of them was:

"The sunlit Censer Peak exhales incense-like cloud;
The cataract hangs like upended stream, sounding loud.
Its torrent dashes three thousand feet from high;
As if the Silver River fell from azure sky."

From his poems we can see how magnificent the mountains and rivers in China are. Indeed, he is such a great poet that his poems were natural, smooth, without being too verbose.

8 李白洞庭葬友的故事

李白之所以在后人眼中具有那么大的魅力，首先在于李白侠肝义胆，重义气，够朋友。他说自己在扬州住了一年，花了30万钱，花这么多钱干什么用啊？都用在救济那些落魄不得志的读书人身上，也就是说自己视金钱如粪土，乐善好施。

有一年，李白出蜀乡，自江陵东下，途经岳阳，再向南去。可是正当他泛舟洞庭湖时，却发生了一件不幸的事情：李白自蜀同来的旅伴吴指南竟暴病身亡。李白悲痛万分，炎热的天气里，他伏在朋友身边，号啕大哭，泪水哭干，哭出鲜血。由于他哭得过于伤痛，路人听到都为之伤心落泪。守尸期间，来了一只猛虎，李白很怕猛虎吃了吴指南的尸体，坚决守在尸体旁不离去。老虎最后可能慑于李白的决心，走了。

旅途上遇到这样的不幸，真是无可奈何。李白只好把吴指南暂时殡葬在洞庭湖边，自己则继续东游，并决心在东南之游归乡以后再来搬运朋友的尸骨。三年后，他从江浙西归，果真返回洞庭湖，从坟墓中挖取吴的遗骸。李白用刀子将尸骨一根根在河中刮洗干净，装进口袋，自己亲自背着这些尸骨披星戴月一路来到江夏（今湖北武昌），借钱将朋友的尸骨在当地重新厚葬。

根据有关专家的研究，李白这种特殊的葬友方式源自南方少数民族的二次捡骨葬法。第一次安葬被称为寄土，可就近安葬；三五年后要开棺捡骨，将骸骨安葬在家族坟地中。李白从小生长的绵州昌隆地区以南，当地人就有二次捡骨葬的风俗。

李白后来在《上安州裴长史书》中详细地描述了他如何用自己的钱救济那些落魄不得志的读书人以及如何悲葬朋友吴指南。

8 Li Bai Buries His Friend beside the Dongting Lake

Why is Li Bai so charming in the eyes of later generations? This is because he was righteous and loyal to his friends. He said he had lived in Yangzhou for a year and used up three hundred thousand Qian silver ingots. Why did he spend so much money? He helped intellectuals and those in need. That is to say, he was so philanthropic-minded that money meant nothing to him.

One year, Li Bai left Shu and went eastward from Jiangling, then went to the south via Yueyang. When he was boating on the Dongting Lake, a misfortune happened: his traveling companion Wu Zhinan, who accompanied him all the way from Shu, died from a sudden illness. Li Bai was so deeply grieved that he bent over his friend's body and burst into tears in the scorching heat. Later, he wept until his tears dried and his blood bled. Passersby all shed tears because his crying was so mournful. When he was protecting his friend's corpse, a fierce tiger came. In fear that the fierce tiger would eat the body of Wu Zhinan, Li Bai resolved to stay beside his friend. Maybe the tiger was afraid of his resolution and it finally left.

Such a misfortune in his traveling made him so helpless. He had no choice but to bury Wu Zhinan beside the Dongting Lake provisionally, and then continued to go eastward. He decided to move his friend's body after coming back from traveling southeast. Three years later, he came back westward from Jiangsu and Zhejiang provinces. As expected, he went back to the Dongting Lake and burrowed out Wu's bones. Then he scraped them one by one in a river with his sword and packed them. He carried all those bones, traveling day and night all the way to Jiangxia (in present Wuchang, Hubei province), then borrowed money to bury his friend again in his hometown with full honour.

According to the researches by relevant experts, Li Bai's unique way of burying his friend originated from minorities in the south with a custom of gathering up bones to bury again. The first time of burying was called consigning to ground, by which a person's body could be buried in a nearby place. Three or five years later, the coffin would be opened and the bones would be collected and buried in their own family tombs. The south of Changlong, Mianzhou, where Li Bai lived since his childhood, was inhabited by aboriginal tribes, which had a custom of gathering up bones to bury again.

Later, in *A Letter to General Secretary Pei*, Li Bai described in detail how he helped those poor intellectuals with his own money and how he buried his friend Wu Zhinan with sorrow.

9 李白江陵幸遇司马承祯的故事

李白没有想到在江陵会有一次不平凡的会见，他居然见到了受三代皇帝崇敬的道士司马承祯。

天台道士司马承帧不仅学得一整套的道家法术，而且写得一手好篆，诗也飘逸如仙。唐玄宗对其非常尊敬，曾将他召至内殿，请教经法，还为他造了阳台观，并派胞妹玉真公主随其学道。

李白能见到这个备受恩宠的道士，自然十分开心，还送上了自己的诗文供其审阅。李白器宇轩昂，资质不凡，司马承祯一见已十分欣赏，及至看了他的诗文，更是惊叹不已，称赞其"有仙风道骨，可与神游八极之表"。因为他看到李白不仅仪表气度非凡，而且才情文章也超人一等，又不汲汲于当世的荣禄仕宦，这是他几十年来在朝在野都没有遇见过的人才，所以他用道家最高的褒奖的话来赞美他。这也就是说他有"仙根"，即有先天成仙的因素，和后来贺知章赞美他是"谪仙人"的意思差不多，都是把他看作非凡之人。这便是李白的风度和诗文的风格给人的总的印象。

李白为司马承祯如此高的评价欢欣鼓舞。他决心去追求"神游八极之表"这样一个永生的、不朽的世界。兴奋之余，他写成大赋《大鹏遇希有鸟赋》，以大鹏自喻，夸写大鹏的庞大迅猛。这是李白最早名扬天下的文章，现抄录如下：

"余昔于江陵，见天台司马子微，谓余有仙风道骨，可与神游八极之表。因著大鹏遇希有鸟赋以自广。此赋已传于世，往往人间见之。悔其少作，未穷宏达之旨，中年弃之。及读晋书，睹阮宣子大鹏赞，鄙心陋之。遂更记忆，多将旧本不同。今复存手集，岂敢传诸作者？庶可示之子弟而已。

其辞曰：南华老仙，发天机于漆园。吐峥嵘之高论，开浩荡之奇言。徵至怪于齐谐，谈北溟之有鱼。吾不知其几千里，其名曰鲲。化成大鹏，质凝胚浑。脱鬐鬣于海岛，张羽毛于天门。刷渤澥之春流，晞扶桑之朝暾。煇赫乎宇宙，凭陵乎昆仑。一鼓一舞，烟朦沙昏。五岳为之震荡，百川为之崩奔。

尔乃蹶厚地，揭太清。亘层霄，突重溟。激三千以崛起，向九万而迅征。背嶪太山之崔嵬，翼举长云之纵横。左回右旋，倏阴忽明。历汗漫以夭矫，羾阊阖之峥嵘。簸鸿蒙，扇雷霆。斗转而天动，山摇而海倾。怒无所搏，雄无所争。固可想像其势，髣髴其形。

若乃足萦虹蜺，目耀日月。连轩沓拖，挥霍翕忽。喷气则六合生云，洒毛则千里飞雪。邈彼北荒，将穷南图。运逸翰以傍击，鼓奔飙而长驱。烛龙衔光以照物，列缺施鞭而启途。块视三山，杯观五湖。其动也神应，其行也道俱。任公见之而罢钓，有穷不敢以弯弧。莫不投竿失镞，仰之长吁。

尔其雄姿壮观，块轧河汉。上摩苍苍，下覆漫漫。盘古开天而直视，羲和倚日以旁叹。缤纷乎八荒之间，掩映乎四海之半。当胸臆之掩画，若混茫之未判。忽腾覆以回转，则霞廓而雾散。

然后六月一息，至于海湄。欻翳景以横翥，逆高天而下垂。憩乎泱漭之野，入乎汪湟之池。猛势所射，馀风所吹。溟涨沸渭，岩峦纷披。天吴为之怵栗，海若为之躨跜。巨鳌冠山而却走，长鲸腾海而下驰。缩壳挫鬣，莫之敢窥。吾亦不测其神怪之若此，盖乃造化之所为。

岂比夫蓬莱之黄鹄，夸金衣与菊裳？耻苍梧之玄凤，耀彩质与锦章。既服御于灵仙，久驯扰于池隍。精卫殷勤于衔木，鶢鶋悲愁乎荐觞。天鸡警晓于蟠桃，踆乌晣耀于太阳。不旷荡而纵适，何拘挛而守常？未若兹鹏之逍遥，无厌类乎比方。不矜大而暴猛，每顺时而行藏。参玄根以比寿，饮元气以充肠。戏旸谷而徘徊，冯炎洲而抑扬。

俄而希有鸟见谓之曰：伟哉鹏乎，此之乐也。吾右翼掩乎西极，左翼蔽乎东荒。跨蹑地络，周旋天纲。以恍惚为巢，以虚无为场。我呼尔游，尔同我翔。于是乎大鹏许之，欣然相随。此二禽已登于寥廓，而斥鷃之辈，空见笑于藩篱。"

现代文译文："我过去在江陵拜会过司马承祯，他说我有仙风道骨，能够和他一起神游八方极远的地方。我故此作《大鹏遇希有鸟赋》以自我安慰。这篇赋已经在世上流传，社会上经常能看到。但我并不满意这年轻时所写的未成熟的作品，感觉它还没有把宏大畅达的中心真正表现出来，中年就丢弃了它。等读到《晋书》，看到阮宣子写的《大鹏赞》，自认为它很粗浅。于是又回想起当年写的《大鹏遇希有鸟赋》来，觉得它和世间流传的旧版本大多不相同。现在又存留手稿本，哪里敢说是传给大家，只是想给子弟们看看罢了。

这赋写道：庄子在漆园发挥他天赋的灵机，口吐不平凡的高论，发出广大旷远的奇言，从齐谐那里收集了非常怪异的事情，谈论北海里的大鱼。我不知道它有几千里长，它的名字叫鲲。鲲化成大鹏，本体就凝结成为浑混的胚胎。在海岛上脱去脊鳍，在天门张开羽毛，迅猛超过流往渤海的春天的河水，急骤胜过朝阳从树梢升起。显赫宇宙之间，高飞超过昆仑。每扇动一次翅膀，烟雾朦胧，沙土飞起，天色都昏暗下来。五岳因它而震动倒塌，百川因为它而冲破堤岸。

在大地上速奔，在太空翱翔，横飞云霄，穿越大海。激荡起三千里的波涛然后突然腾空而起，向着那九万里的高空疾飞而去。高耸的背脊就像巍峨的大山，扇动的翅膀就像纵横连绵的云。一会向左旋转，一会向右盘旋，顷刻间消失了身影，眨眼间又出现在天上。它以矫健的身姿穿越漫无边际的天空，飞经险峻的高山而到达天门。上下俯冲，摇动大海云气，扇动翅膀，传出震雷声声，星斗转移而上天震动，高山摇晃而大海倾翻。没有什么敢和它搏击称雄，没有什么敢和它竞争。由此可以想象它的气势和大概的情形。

至于它爪子周围环绕着虹霓，眼睛里闪耀着日月般的光芒。飞舞盘旋，迅疾倏忽。喷口气，天地四方就会生出云彩；抖动一下羽毛，方圆千里之内就会飞起漫天雪花。它从遥远的北方准备往南方飞行。有时挥动强健的翅膀以侧旋，有时腾起狂风而直飞。烛龙神口衔宝物为它照亮万物，闪电挥舞长鞭为它开路。三山在它看来就是几个土块，五湖在它眼里就是一杯水。它一动就会有神相应，它一飞就会有道相从。任公子看见它停止了垂钓，有穷氏不敢弯弓放箭。他们掷下鱼竿、丢弃箭杆，仰天看着它发出无奈的长叹。

至于它勇盛的姿态、雄壮的形象，像是一眼望不到边际，掩映着整个银河。向上磨蹭着苍天，向下覆盖着大地。开天的盘古瞪着眼，直愣愣地望着它不知如何是好，羲和靠在日头旁边发出声声叹息。八方荒远的地方都能感受到它盛大的气势,大半个天下都被它遮盖住了。它的胸脯对着太阳就挡住了光线,如同黑夜降临,一片模糊,什么东西都难以分辨。突然间身体翻飞而回转过来,立刻霞光普照,云雾也消散了。

然后,每隔六个月的时间它就到海边歇息一次。忽然间,它高举奋飞,遮蔽了日月的光辉,从天而降时巨大的身形向下垂挂着。在广大无边的原野上休息,有时进入深广的湖水。它迅猛的气势喷射到的地方,大海翻腾奔涌;余风吹过的地方,高峻的山峦一片散乱。水神天吴看到后惊恐不安,海神海若畏惧得一动不敢动。头脑像山一样的巨鳌退避跑开,腾飞在大海上的长鲸往下游飞驰。至于其他生物,有的把头缩进壳中,有的收缩鬣毛,恐惧得连看都不敢看大鹏一眼。我也没有料想它的神奇怪异能到这种程度,这大约是大自然所创造的吧。

大鹏难道能和那个待在蓬莱岛上的黄鹄相比,让人去夸耀金饰装点的上衣和菊花做成的下衣?大鹏耻于学苍梧山上的凤凰,去炫耀自己羽毛上彩色的质地和美丽的花纹。这些禽鸟,有的早已经被神仙役使,有的长久而顺服地生活在护城河的小水沟中。精卫勤劳地衔着树枝填海,鹦鹉对着人们敬献的美酒发出悲哀的叫声。天鸡在蟠桃树上报晓,三足乌在太阳中发出光辉。它们不能在旷远无边的地方随心所欲地表现性情,为什么竟这样拘泥地固守常规呢?它们都个不如优游自得的这只大鹏,没有任何东西能够和大鹏相比。大鹏从不骄矜尊大而凶狠暴戾,每每顺应时宜,调整自己的行止。领悟道的根本以比较寿数多少,饮用天地未分前的混沌之气来充饥。在太阳升起的地方游戏,从容而安逸飞行;倚托南海一带炎热的岛屿,扬扬而自得。

不久,希有鸟看见了大鹏,它对大鹏说:'大鹏你真伟大啊,这真是让我高兴的事。我右边的翅膀能覆盖西方极远之处,我的左翼能遮挡东方极远之处。跨越疆域的界限,盘桓上天的纲维。以恍惚作为巢穴,把虚无当成场地。我呼唤你同游,你和我一起飞翔吧。'大鹏于是答应了它的要求,高兴地随它飞去。这两只鸟都已经飞上了辽阔的天空,而那些斥鷃一类的小鸟,因囿于自己的见识,而徒自对它们发出嘲笑。"①

---

① 英文对照中按现代文译文翻译,后同。

9 Li Bai Fortunately Meets Sima Chengzhen in Jiangling

Beyond his expectation, Li Bai had such an extraordinary experience in Jiangling that he met Taoist Sima Chengzhen who was respected by three generations of emperors.

Sima Chengzhen, Tiantai Taoist, not only learned Taoism scriptures, but also wrote beautiful small seal characters and elegant poems. So he was greatly respected by Emperor Xuanzong who once invited him to the adytum to teach Taoism. What's more, Emperor Xuanzong built Yangtai Taoist Temple for him, and sent his sister Princess Yuzhen to learn from him.

Li Bai was so delighted to meet this Taoist who was in special favour of the emperor, so he presented his poems to Sima. Li Bai, a handsome man with great talent, was extremely appreciated by Sima Chengzhen at first sight. When reading Li Bai's poems, Sima marvelled and acclaimed him "with such a sage-like person, I would like to travel through time and space". He praised Li Bai so highly because Li Bai not only had an impressive appearance, possessed great talent which was beyond those of many ordinary people, but also disdained wealth and rank. In his eyes, Li Bai had such a "gene for immortal" that he was destined to be an immortal, which has the same meaning with "Demoted Immortal" praised by He Zhizhang who regarded Li Bai as an eminent person. This is the general impression made of Li Bai's manner and poems.

Li Bai was extremely inspired by Sima's praise, thus he determined to pursue an eternal world of "traveling through time and space". With excitement, he wrote a poem named *A Roc Met a Rare Bird* to praise roc's great figure and swiftness. This is the earliest article that made him world-famous. We copy the following:

"I paid a visit to Sima Chengzhen in Jiangling who said that I was a sage-like person, so he wanted to travel through time and space with me. Therefore I wrote *A Roc Met a Rare Bird* to comfort myself. And this prose poem was spread among people, and became a major hit at that time. However, I was not satisfied with my jerky work made in my young age, which did not fully express its grand main idea, so I abandoned it in my middle age. Until reading *Book of the Jin Dynasties* and *Eulogy of Roc* made by Ruan Xuanzi, I still thought my work was superficial. Then I recalled what I had written, *A Roc Met a Rare Bird*, which was different from those versions spread among people. Until now, I have kept this manuscript just for our young generations to have a look. How did I dare to pass it to you?

It said: Zhuangzi presented his inborn talent, talked with eloquence and expressed himself strangely in Qiyuan. He also collected something odd from Qi Xie and talked about the big fish in the North Sea. I do not know how long the fish is, but I know its name 'Kun'. Kun changed into a roc, so its original body congealed into a mixed embryo. It lost its dorsal fin, and opened its wings at the sky gate. It flew in the sky more swiftly and violently than the spring flowing river to the Bohai Sea, more abruptly than the morning rising sun from a tree. So impressive in the expansive space, it flew higher than the Kunlun Mountains. Every time it flapped its wings, the sky would be darkened with smoky and hazy feather and flying dust. Because of it, the Five Mountains shook and collapsed, and hundreds of rivers broke their levees.

It ran fast on the earth and flew freely in the sky, making its figure all over up in the sky and down in the sea. Surging on a vast expanse of great waves, then it soared to thousands of miles up in the sky. Its towering dorsal fin was like a lofty mountain, its flapping wings as rolling clouds. In one minute, it hovered to the left, and then to the right. All of a sudden, it disappeared, and in a blink, it appeared in the sky. With a vigorous posture, it traversed the boundless sky, arriving at the sky gate after passing through steep mountains. Diving up and down, it shook the mist on the sea. Flapping its wings, it made thunderous noise. It made stars move, the sky shake, mountains rock and seas surge. Nobody dared to fight with it, and no one dared to compete with it. Therefore, you can imagine its imposing manner.

Its claws were surrounded by a rainbow and its eyes shone with sunlight and moonlight. Flying and hovering from the remote north to the south, it moved swiftly. Breathing a breath, it would arouse clouds everywhere. Flapping its wings, it would cause snowflakes to dance within thousands of miles. The god of candle dragon gagged its mouth with treasure to light up everything for it, and the lightning waved a long whip to open a way for it. In its eyes, the three mountains were just blocks of soil, and the five lakes were just a glass of water. Once it moved, god would help him; once it flew, Taoists would follow it. Once seeing it, a noble man from Ren would stop fishing at once, and tribe of You Qiong dared not to shoot. They put down their fishing rods and arrows, looking up at the sky and heaving a deep sigh.

Its brave and magnificent figure was huge and endless, shrouding the whole Milky Way. Up it rubbed the sky, and down it covered the Earth. Pan Gu, the man who created the world, stared at it and did not know how to deal with it; and Xi He, leaning on the sun, heaved sighs continuously. Even in the remotest place, its grand vigour could be realised, with its breast facing the sun, blanketing and obscuring the day like nightfall. All of a sudden, it turned around, making the sun shine and the mist disappear.

Then, every six months, it would fly to the seaside for a rest. Suddenly, it soared up, covering the light of the sun and the moon. While it dropped from the sky, its figure plummeted down. It rested on an expansive campagna, and sometimes it dived into a deep lake. When its grand momentum emitting from itself, the sea would surge. When the remaining winds blew, the lofty mountains would be in a mess. Tian Wu, the god of water, felt anxious after seeing it. And Hai Ruo, the god of sea, was afraid to move. A huge legendary turtle, whose brain is as big as a mountain, once meeting it, would flee away at once. The largest whale would begin to swim downstream after seeing it. And other creatures—some retracting their heads into their shells, and some retracting their manes, dared not to take a look at the roc. I also did not expect it to be so miraculous and monstrous. Maybe nature made it.

Could we compare the roc with the yellow swan living on Penglai Island? The latter let people flatter its gold-decorated clothes and chrysanthemum-made pants. The former disdained the phoenix living in Mount Cangwu which liked showing off its colourful feathers and beautiful patterns. These birds, some had been enslaved by immortals, and some had been tamed to live in the ditches of moats. Jing Wei, craming her mouth with branches, was busy with filling up the sea. Yuanju, a kind of seabird, whined when people toasted it. Chickens over sky heralded the break of a day in a peach tree. The three-legged crow showed its shining image in the sun. All of them could not express their true temperament in boundless places. Then why did they stick to their routines? They were inferior to the free roc. So nothing could place on a par with this roc. However, the roc never felt high and mighty, or never showed a fierce and violence image. It often adjusted itself according to different situations. It tried to comprehend the essence of Taoism to compare how long the lifetime is, and it ate chaos before the separation of Earth and Heaven. It played where the sun rises, flying unhurriedly. On torrid islands in the South China Sea, it lived a leisurely life.

Soon, the rare bird saw the roc and said: 'How great you are! I am so glad to see that. My right wing could cover the remotest place in the west, and my left wing in the east. I could traverse boundaries and fly beyond the rules of heaven. I could build my nest with trance, and use nihility as my stage. I would like to invite you to fly with me!' The roc said yes and flew with it happily. The two birds flew to the broad sky, while those sparrows laughed at them because of their limited knowledge."

10 李白拜谒李邕的故事

李白在江夏停留到阳春三月，终于等到了在东都任员外司马的李邕。

李邕，祖籍广陵（今江苏扬州），后迁至江夏，住在鄂州城外的小洪山下。他既是高居四品的大官，又是当代名士。李邕的父亲李善在武则天时期曾擢崇贤馆直学士、沛王侍读，为《文选》作注，又撰《汉书辨惑》30卷。李邕秉承家学，自幼刻苦攻读诗书和书法。他在洪山上凿有石室，是他少年时代刻苦磨砺自己的地方。他的事迹在江夏广为流传，而他的书法乃当时数一数二的大家之作，人们为求他的墨宝和他撰写的碑铭不远万里和不惜万金。李邕怀有大才，他任职的地方都有供人赞美的佳绩，喜爱文学才士，亦喜奖掖后进，但他恃才傲物，桀骜不驯，不见容于朝廷，曾数度在朝中任职又数度被排斥到外地。他能在东都任职，还是老宰相宋璟极为赏识他的才华，开元七年（719年），将他从括州司马调任渝州（今重庆）刺史，迅又调到东都任员外司马。李邕每年清明必回江夏扫墓祭祖，而江夏士子却早在盼望着，希望能一识他的尊颜，甚或能获得他的教益。

李白十分兴奋，他对李邕的声名十分景仰。他读过李邕的文章，到江夏后又亲睹李邕高妙的书艺，由衷地想能有机会拜谒，获得他在诗文和书法上的指点和教导。他早早准备好了诗文，在李邕回江夏的次日就投递了进去。

李白获得了接见。李邕对李白亦有耳闻，他在任渝州刺史时，宰相苏颋被贬到益州（今成都）任长史，曾向朝廷推荐过李白的文章，此事在巴蜀之地反响强烈。他接到李白的拜帖，便于夜深人静客人散后认真地翻阅起来。他十分赞赏李白的诗文，特别是李白出川以来一路所写的诗歌，可谓吸收了各地民歌的精华，并在原有基础上升华和再创造，《峨眉山月歌》《巴女词》《荆州歌》《江夏行》等道出了各地的风土民情，热情讴歌了他们的生产生活和爱情，此子不愧文采非凡，但从《明堂赋》《大鹏遇希有鸟赋》中既看出此子才华横溢，志向宏伟，又看出好加卖弄和狂妄。李邕久久吟诵，击节叹赏。他想，明日在接见李白时先严厉批评，让他日后不要太张狂，戒去浮躁的心理，然后鼓励他博学多思。如此发展下去，日后必为我大唐文坛上的奇葩。

"学生拜见李大人。"李白在李邕家仆的引领下进入李府中堂，见李邕端坐于大堂之上，便深深拜揖下去。

李邕见李白进门只揖不跪，心中立时大为震怒：这小子太狂妄了！身为朝廷四品命官，又是当今名士，谁人见之不惧、不跪？李邕压制住心头的怒火，厉声问道："来者何事？"

李白天性高傲，与朋友相处总待以平等之礼，参谒官员，从来只揖不跪，也因此得罪了许多贵人。但李白的原则是：既然是以文会友，相互切磋，就不应有高低贵贱之分。李白知道李邕因自己不跪而恼怒，心中极度失望，见李邕斥问，便抬头抗声答道："学生素闻大人高名，心中仰慕已久，得知大人回乡扫墓祭祖，学生亦正好游历到此地，故特来拜见，想聆听大人的指点和教诲。"

"岂敢！足下年少才俊，非老夫能妄加评判。家中还有些许小事待理。送客！"

李白手捧退回的诗文手稿，从李府走出，心中极度伤心、愤怒和失望。他没有料到，性格虽然十分古怪但却非常爱才的李邕大人竟如此轻视自己，因为一个真正爱才的人是不会因自己的不跪而断然排斥自己的。李白极为愤怒，他想：上天既然将我降生于世，我就一定会做出一番伟业来！不达自己理想决不罢休。回到馆舍，李白奋笔疾书，写下《上李邕》一诗：

"大鹏一日同风起，扶摇直上九万里。

假令风歇时下来，犹能簸却沧溟水。

时人见我恒殊调，闻余大言皆冷笑。

宣父犹能畏后生，丈夫未可轻年少。"

在这首诗中，李白再次以大鹏自负。他在向世人昭示：他的"书剑报明时"的志愿一定要达到！当天，李白让人将此诗送到李府，送给李邕大人。

10 Li Bai Visits Li Yong

Looking forward to visiting Li Yong, who served as the Yuanwai Sima in Dongdu, Li Bai stayed at Jiangxia until March and finally met Li Yong.

Li Yong was born in Jiangxia, but his native place is in Guangling (present Yangzhou, Jiangsu province). Li Yong lived at the foot of Mount Hong outside the city of E'zhou. He was the fourth-grade official and also a famous scholar at that time. His father, Li Shan, served as an official in Chongxian Academy and the study assistant of Prince Pei in the Zhou Dynasty. He made notes for *The Selection of Literary* and wrote 30 chapters of *The Analysis of the History of the Former Han Dynasty*. Li Yong inherited his family culture and worked hard at poetry and Chinese calligraphy since he was a child. He had a stone chamber on Mount Hong, where he assiduously forged his talents. His stories were spread far and wide in Jiangxia and he was also a distinguished calligrapher. People were willing to spend a very long time to find him and a large amount of money to buy his calligraphic works and inscriptions. Li Yong had great talents and achieved much in his official career. He appreciated literary scholars and always encouraged young scholars. However, he was too arrogant to get along with other officials who served in the royal court. So he was repelled by them and was appointed to different places far away from the capital. Thanks to Song Jing, an old prime minister who appreciated Li Yong's talents very much, he could get the position in Dongdu. In the 7th year of Kaiyuan (719 A.D.), Li Yong was transferred to be Cishi of Yuzhou (present Chongqing) and then retransferred to be Yuanwai Sima in Dongdu. On every Tomb-Sweeping Day, when Li Yong came back to Jiangxia, his hometown, to sweep tombs and worship his ancestors, scholars in Jiangxia gathered, looking forward to meeting him.

Li Bai was so thrilled because he had admired Li Yong for a long time. He had read Li Yong's articles before and witnessed his spectacular calligraphy in Jiangxia. He sincerely hoped that he could have a chance to visit Li Yong and obtain some advice about poetry and calligraphy from him. Therefore, he prepared his poem in advance and delivered it to him the next day after Li Yong's arrival.

Finally, Li Bai gained the permission to visit Li Yong, who had also heard about him long before. When Li Yong served as Cishi of Yuzhou, Su Ting, the prime minister who had been banished to Yizhou(present Chengdu), had ever recommended Li Bai's poems to the emperor, which received enormous responses among people who lived in Ba and Shu. After receiving Li Bai's visiting card, Li Yong read it thoroughly at night. He appreciated Li Bai's poems, especially his folk poems written after he left Sichuan, which assimilated the essence of folk songs from different regions. Also, these poems are great recreations of the originals. *The Moon over the Mount Emei, Song of a Woman of Ba, Song of Jingzhou* and *The Journey in Jiangxia* tell us the local customs and conditions in various regions and they also eulogise people's zest of life and love. These poems show that Li Bai really had extraordinary talent and ambition. However, from *Ode of The Mingtang* and *The Roc Met a Rare Bird,* Li Yong learned that although Li Bai was talented, he was also conceited and liked showing off his talent. He recited his poems many times and tapped his hand (in compliment). He thought that he should criticise Li Bai for his arrogance at first, then advise him to get rid of this fickle mind and encourage him to read and think more. He was also sure that only if Li Bai followed his instructions, could he rise as a miracle in the literature world of the Tang Dynasty.

"I am Li Bai. I came here to visit you." Having been led by Li Yong's servant, Li Bai came to Li Yong's residence, only to see Li Yong sitting in the hall. Then, Li Bai made a bow with his hands folding in front.

Li Yong was so angry because Li Bai did not kneel down but only bowed. Li Yong thought: "What an arrogant young man!" Li Yong was a fourth-grade official in the royal court and a famous scholar. Of course everyone who saw him would be afraid of him and kneel down. Li Yong restrained his anger and asked sharply: "What do you come here for?"

Li Bai was born proud and always treated his friends equally. When he met officials, he always bowed but was unwilling to kneel down. Because of this, he offended many officials. However, Li Bai had his own principle: since they made friends by writing poems, exchanging views and learning from each other, they should abandon their hierarchical thoughts and rites. Therefore, Li Bai felt so disappointed with Li Yong that he headed up and answered Li Yong's ironic scolding in an aggrieved mood: "I have heard of you long time ago and really admire you. This time I heard about your return and coincidently I have just been here. So I came here to meet you and hoped that you could give me some instructions."

"I dare not, I have no instructions for you! You are so talented that I dare not to comment on you. As I have some trivia to deal with right now, I have to say goodbye."

Later, Li Yong returned the poem script to Li Bai. After walking out of Li Yong's residence, Li Bai felt angry, deeply depressed and disappointed. He had not expect that Li Yong, who was strange but also thirsty for talented scholars, despised him to that extent. He thought that a man who really loved talent would not dislike him because of his refusal to kneel down. He was so angry and thought: "Heaven has made us talents, and we were not made in vain. I would not give up until I realize my ideals!" After coming back to the inn, he wrote a poem *To Li Yong*:

"If once together with the wind the roc could rise,
He would fly ninety thousand *li* up to the skies.
E'en if he must descend when the wind has abated,
Still billows will be raised and the sea agitated.
Seeing me, those in power think I'm rather queer;
Hearing me freely talk, they can't refrain from sneer.
Confucius was in dread of talents that would be;

A sage will ne'er look down upon a youth like me."

In this poem, Li Bai compared himself to the roc. He wanted to tell people that his dream of "devoting all my talents to great times" would definitely come true. On the very day, Li Bai had this poem sent to Li Yong.

11 李白被称为"天上谪仙人"的故事

李白被称为"天上谪仙人",意思是从天上降到人间的仙人。这是著名诗人贺知章对李白的称誉。

李白是唐代杰出的诗人,他青少年时代在蜀地度过。蜀地雄奇秀丽的山水陶冶了他的情思,成为他诗歌创作的源泉,奠定了他浪漫的文学风格。他志向远大,不局限于一隅之地,从翻越险峻的蜀道来到京师长安。

刚到长安,李白住在馆舍里。当时已是诗名远扬的太子宾客秘书监贺知章,久闻李白的诗名,前来馆舍看望他。贺知章见李白后,被李白秀丽的姿容吸引住了,赞不绝口,认为他是非常之人。接着,贺知章提出要看李白写的诗,李白取出《蜀道难》一篇呈给他看。

"噫吁嚱,危乎高哉!

蜀道之难,难于上青天!

蚕丛及鱼凫,开国何茫然!

尔来四万八千岁,不与秦塞通人烟。

西当太白有鸟道,可以横绝峨眉巅。

地崩山摧壮士死,然后天梯石栈相钩连。

上有六龙回日之高标,下有冲波逆折之回川。

黄鹤之飞尚不得过,猿猱欲度愁攀援。

青泥何盘盘,百步九折萦岩峦。

扪参历井仰胁息，以手抚膺坐长叹。
问君西游何时还，畏途巉岩不可攀。
但见悲鸟号古木，雄飞雌从绕林间。
又闻子规啼夜月，愁空山。
蜀道之难，难于上青天，使人听此凋朱颜。
连峰去天不盈尺，枯松倒挂倚绝壁。
飞湍瀑流争喧豗，砯崖转石万壑雷。
其险也若此，嗟尔远道之人胡为乎来哉！
剑阁峥嵘而崔嵬，一夫当关，万夫莫开。
所守或匪亲，化为狼与豺。
朝避猛虎，夕避长蛇，磨牙吮血，杀人如麻。
锦城虽云乐，不如早还家。
蜀道之难，难于上青天，侧身西望长咨嗟！"

当时的贺知章已年逾古稀，李白的《蜀道难》却激起了心如古井的贺知章的感情狂澜，贺知章被这首诗的气势及神奇的想象震住了，一边吟诵，一边赞叹说："你果然是太白金星下凡，凡夫俗子哪里能写得出这样的好诗来呢？"最后，他竖起大拇指对李白说："你莫不是天上下凡的谪仙人（意思是受到责罚降到人间来的仙人）吧，只有天上的神仙才能写出这样绝妙的诗句！"贺知章认为此诗只有神仙才写得出来，因而称李白为"谪仙人"，即从天上下来的仙人。可见对李白评价之高。贺知章是文坛元老，《蜀道难》得到他如此推许，所以，不久之后，李白这首诗连同"谪仙人"的名号就传遍天下。而李白也自称为"青莲居士谪仙人"。

贺知章初见李白，十分投契，大有相见恨晚之感，就把他引为知音。黄昏时分，贺知章邀请李白去饮酒，在酒店刚坐下，才想起身边没有带钱。他想了想，立刻解下身上佩带的金龟，呼唤店家换来美酒。李白阻拦说："使不得，这是皇家按品级给你的饰品，怎好拿来换酒呢？"贺知章仰面大笑说："这算得了什么？今日有幸与仙人结友，可要喝个痛快！区区金龟哪能妨碍我俩一同享乐呢？"二人开怀畅饮，一醉方休。

贺知章是当世知名诗人，又在朝廷任官，一般人想结交也结交不上。李白得到贺知章的如此厚待，他的诗就更出名了。不久，贺知章又读到李白的新作《乌栖曲》：

"姑苏台上乌栖时，吴王宫里醉西施。

吴歌楚舞欢未毕，青山欲衔半边日。

银箭金壶漏水多，起看秋月坠江波。

东方渐高奈乐何！"

贺知章叹赏不已，兴奋地说："这诗真可以感动鬼神了。"后来，贺知章向皇帝推荐李白，皇帝也已久闻李白大名，于是就任命李白为翰林学士。

后来贺知章去世，李白独自对酒，怅然有怀，想起当年金龟换酒，便写下《对酒忆贺监二首并序》：

太子宾客贺公。于长安紫极宫一见余，呼余为"谪仙人"，因解金龟换酒为乐。殁后对酒。怅然有怀，而作是诗。

其一

四明有狂客，风流贺季真。

长安一相见，呼我谪仙人。

昔好杯中物，翻为松下尘。

金龟换酒处，却忆泪沾中。

其二

狂客归四明，山阴道士迎。

敕赐镜湖水，为君台沼荣。

人亡余故宅，空有荷花生。

念此杳如梦，凄然伤我情。

贺知章金龟换酒与李白畅饮，后人引为旷达酣饮、倾心结交的典故，宋代刘望之《水调歌头·劝子一杯酒》词中云："谪仙人，千金龟，换美酒。"后来，"谪仙人"这一典故用来指李白，也用以泛指潇洒飘逸、才华横溢的诗人、作家。

11 Li Bai, Known as the "Demoted Immortal"

Li Bai was called the "Demoted Immortal", which means the immortal who was sent from heaven to earth. It was a compliment by He Zhizhang, a famous poet of his time.

Li Bai lived in Shu when he was a teenager. Magnificent and beautiful landscapes there influenced his sentiment and thought. They are also the source of his poetic creation and the foundation of his romantic style. He had great ambitions and was reluctant to confine himself to his hometown, so he crossed high mountains in Shu and arrived in Chang'an, the capital city of the Tang Dynasty.

Once arriving in Chang'an, he settled at an inn. At that time, He Zhizhang was a famous and brilliant poet, who served as a guest and Mishujian under the prince. He heard of Li Bai's prestige, so he paid a visit to Li Bai. At first sight, he was attracted by Li Bai's temperament and appearance. He praised him and thought Li Bai was not an ordinary person. Later he asked Li Bai to show him some poems. Then Li Bai presented his masterpiece *Hard Is the Road to Shu*:

"Oho! Behold! How steep! How high!
The road to Shu is harder than to climb the sky.
Since the two pioneers,
Put the kingdom in order,
Have passed forty-eight thousand years,
And few have tried to pass its border.
There's a bird track o'er Great White Mountain to the west,
Which cuts through Mount Emei by the crest.
The crest crumbled, five serpent-killing heroes slain,

Along the cliffs a rocky path was hacked then.

Above stand peaks too high for the sun to pass o'er;

Below the torrents run back and forth, churn and roar.

Even the Golden Crane can't fly across;

How to climb over, gibbons are at a loss.

What tortuous mountain path Green Mud Ridge faces!

Around the top we turn nine turns each hundred paces.

Looking up breathless, I can touch the stars nearby;

Beating my breast, I sink on the ground with long sigh.

When will you come back from this journey to the west?

How can you climb up dangerous path and mountain crest,

Where you can hear on ancient trees but sad birds wail

And see the female birds fly, followed by the male?

And hear homo-going cuckoos weep.

Beneath the moon in mountains deep?

The road to Shu is harder than to climb the sky,

On hearing this, your cheeks would lose their rosy dye.

Between the sky and peaks there is not a foot's space,

And ancient pines hang, head-down, from the cliff's surface,

And cataracts and torrents dash on boulders under,

Roaring like thousands of echoes of thunder.

So dangerous these places are,

Alas! why should you come here from afar?

Rugged is the path between the cliffs so steep and high,

Guarded by one,

And forced by none.

Disloyal guards,

Would turn wolves and pards,

Man-eating tigers at daybreak

And at dusk blood-sucking long snake.

One may make merry in the Town of Silk, I know,

But I would rather homeward go.

The road to Shu is harder than to climb the sky,

I'd turn and, westward look with long, long sigh."

At that time, He Zhizhang was over 70 years old and became calm and quiet about everything. However, this poem aroused his passion. Totally shocked by the astonishing momentum and imagination of this poem, he heaped praise upon Li Bai: "You are really a demoted immortal from paradise! Nobody else could create such a great poem like this!" He raised his thumb to Li Bai and called him demoted immortal, which means relegated immortal from heaven to earth. Gaining such high esteem and appreciation from a senior poet, Li Bai called himself "Demoted Immortal of Buddhist Qinglian". Soon afterwards, this poem and his alias "Immortal" spread worldwide.

When He Zhizhang met Li Bai for the first time, he got along well with him, but had a feeling of meeting him too late. So he regarded Li Bai as his confidant and invited him to drink together. When they sat down in an inn at dusk, He Zhizhang realised he had not brought money with him. He wanted to exchange his golden accessories for some wine. Li Bai stopped him and said: "It is an imperial ornament showing your official rank and you shouldn't exchange it for wine." He Zhizhang laughed and said: "It means nothing compared with my friend. Today I had a great honour to make friends with you demoted immortal; of course we should definitely drink to our heart's content! How can a shabby seal prevent us from enjoying ourselves." So, they both had a hearty drink until they got drunk.

At that time, He Zhizhang was a famous poet who served in the royal court. It's hard for a common person to associate with him. So, after being entertained by He Zhizhang, Li Bai became more famous for his poems. Soon He Zhizhang read his new work *Crows Going Back to Their Nest*:

"O'er Royal Terrace when crows flew back to their nest,
The king in Royal Palace feast'd his mistress drunk.
The Southern maidens sang and danced without rest.
Till beak-like mountain-peaks would peck the sun half-sunk.
The golden clepsydra could not stop water's flow,
O'r river waves the autumn moon was hanging low.
But wouldn't the king enjoy his in Eastern glow?"

He Zhizhang appreciated and praised Li Bai's poem and said with excitement: "Even the ghosts and immortals will be moved by this poem!" Later, He Zhizhang recommended Li Bai to the emperor who had heard of Li Bai's reputation long time before. Because of this, Li Bai was appointed as the Hanlin Scholar at the Imperial Academy.

Some time later, He Zhizhang passed away. When Li Bai was drinking alone, he thought of He Zhizhang, who exchanged his golden accessories for wine. Therefore, Li Bai wrote the poem *In Memoriam* (*The poet mourns He Zhizhang*).

In this poem, Li Bai wrote:

"He Zhizhang was a guest who worked for the Crown Prince. When we met at the Ziji Palace in Chang'an for the first time, he called me 'demoted immortal'. He exchanged his golden accessories for wine. After he passed away, I drank wine alone and wrote this poem when thinking of him.

I

There was an unrestrained person who lived at the Mount Siming,
His name was He Jizhen.
The first time we met in Chang'an,
He called me celestial being from the paradise.
He was an immortal, who loved wine,
But now passed away and became the dust under the pine.
He used his official seal to exchange wine for us.

Every time I cry with tears when thinking of him.

II

When He Zhizhang came back to the Mount Siming,

Local Taoist priests in Shan Yin got together to welcome his arrival.

The Lake of Jing, a beautiful mountain,

He enjoyed such sceneries.

The man passed away,

Leaving his former residence there and lotus in the lake.

Vague images in lifetime are just like a great dream,

Hurting my feeling deeply."

The story that He Zhizhang exchanged his golden accessories for wine was regarded as an allusion. Liu Wangzhi, a poet in the Song Dynasty, wrote a poem titled *Prelude to Water Melody*. The line "Golden accessories exchanged good wine for Demoted Immortal" talks about this story. Later, Li Bai became known as the "Demoted Immortal", which can also be used to refer to elegant and talented poets or writers.

12 李白白兆山"洗脚塘"的故事

昔时 ·位云游高僧来到湖北安陆烟店，见一座山上霞光普照，紫气升腾，沾有神灵之气，便为它取名叫"白兆山"。后来李白仗剑骑马出游来到白兆山顿有所悟，感慨道："山曰为白兆，始知李白来。"李白就此在安陆定居10年。

安陆有个不学无术、胸无点墨的县官，却又贪赃枉法投机钻营，一心想要升官发财。这一年皇帝要考核县官，诗写得好的升官，差者削职。

县官慌乱不安，后来还是那位衙役出主意，请居住在白兆山的李白来

代笔作诗。县官立刻宴请李白，酒过数巡后，县官请求李白代写诗赋去应试并许诺厚报。李白听后才知县官并非钦慕自己之诗才，心中恼怒，冷冷地说："不敢从命，另请高明。"便拂袖而去。

在回家的路上李白越想越窝囊越气恼，县衙应是清白之地，却被这些俗不可耐的官吏弄得如此龌龊不堪，今天算瞎了眼竟然走到那里把我的脚都弄脏了，李白边走边想，发现前面有口方塘，塘里的水十分干净，便急忙跳下马坐在塘边，在清水中使劲地洗着双脚。约莫洗了一个时辰，方直起身长舒一口气，上马回到白兆山家里。

后人对李白蔑视权臣，不被人所用的品格非常敬佩，就把他洗过脚的地方取名为"洗脚塘"。

12 Li Bai and the "Foot-Bathing Pond" near Mount Baizhao

Once, an eminent monk traveled to Yandian town, Anlu, Hubei province. When he saw a mountain lit by the sun and surrounded with violet haze, he thought that there was an aura of divinity. Therefore, he named it "Mount Baizhao". Afterwards, when riding to Mount Baizhao on horseback with his sword, he sighed with sudden enlightenment: "This mountain was named Baizhao because it knew that Li Bai would come here one day." So, he made a settlement in Anlu for 10 years.

In Anlu, there was an ignorant county magistrate. He not only speculated and took bribes, but also wished to get promoted and gain prosperity through speculation. One year, the emperor wanted to test those county magistrates, and promised that he would promote those who wrote great poems, whilst others would be demoted.

The county magistrate was in deep panic. A staff member in *yamen* made a suggestion that he should ask Li Bai, who lived in Mount Baizhao, to write poems for him. Very soon, the county magistrate held a banquet in honour of Li Bai. After drinking for a while, he told Li Bai about his intention and promised him generous rewards. Realizing that the county magistrate did not admire his poetic talent, he felt irritated and said indifferently: "That job is beyond my competence, so please find a better one." Then he went away in a huff.

On the way home, Li Bai got more annoyed, thinking that the county *yamen* should have been a fair place, but now it was polluted by vulgar officials. "How blind I was today, and my feet was stained when I went there." Li Bai thought to himself over walking, and then found a clean pond, so he quickly jumped down from his horse and sat beside it washing his feet carefully. After about two hours, he got up with a long sigh of relief, then he returned to his horse and went back home in Mount Baizhao.

The later generations thought highly of Li Bai, who despised the power and was unwilling to be taken advantage of by others. Therefore, they named this place where Li Bai bathed his feet "Foot-Bathing Pond".

13 李白白兆山"下马桩"的故事

李白外出漫游归来，才骑马回到白兆山家里，贤惠的许氏夫人总要去村口替丈夫牵马。

一日，许氏夫人见李白骑着马志得意满地回来，许夫人迎上前去笑着说："你又作了什么好诗，念给我听听吧！"李白在马背上望了夫人一眼前仰后合地吟道：

"昔日横波目，今为流泪泉。

不信妾肠断，归来看取明镜前。"

李白吟罢，孤芳自赏地笑望着相门淑女，谁知夫人不以为然地笑了笑说："以前当你骑马回家时，我都到这里接你。"李白赶紧说："夫人若能指出我刚才吟的诗有前人鸿爪，今后回来到此下马回家。"

许氏夫人对李白说："君不闻武后诗乎？"

许氏夫人吟出武后的诗句"不信比来常下泪，开箱验取石榴裙"。吟完就把手中的缰绳递还给李白，说："你自己牵着吧。"李白听了后"爽然若失"，对夫人说："我只知你面如桃花，却不知你胸藏锦绣。"

从此以后，李白到这个石柱边就下马走回家，后人就给这个石柱取名"下马桩"。

13 Li Bai and the "Dismounting Stake"

Every time Li Bai returned from his travels and rode his horse home to Mount Baizhao, his virtuous wife Xu would always run to the entrance of the village, and take his horse home.

One day, seeing Li Bai coming back home full of pride on his horse, Xu stepped forward and smiled: "Why not chant your wonderful new poems to me?" Li Bai took a glance at his wife and chanted, rolling with laughter:

"Bright eyes in the past, spring of dripping tears at present.

Doubt my deep affliction; why not take a look at my face before mirror?"

Li Bai stopped and gazed at his wife with admiration, but his wife ignored him and smiled: "In the past, every time you came home riding a horse, I would come here to welcome you." Li Bai said promptly: "If you were to point out the ancient reference in this poem, I would go home on foot."

His wife Xu said to him: "Haven't you ever heard about the poem by Empress Wu?"

Then she chanted the poem: "Doubt that I shed tears for you, why not open the box to see whether my red dress was brimmed with tears." After chanting, she passed the rein in her hand to Li Bai, refusing to take the horse for him anymore. Li Bai felt lost and said to his wife: "What I know is your face is as beautiful as a rose, but what I don't know is your talent."

From that day on, Li Bai would dismount from his horse at the stone stake and went home on foot. Therefore, it was named "Dismounting Stake" by later generations.

14 诗仙李白与酒的故事

自古文人墨客、迁客骚人，多半好酒，演绎千古传奇。王羲之醉酒《兰亭序》名世，张旭酒后狂草惊人，李白斗酒诗百篇……

今天，我们说的是诗仙亦酒仙的李白的故事。曾有诗曰《李白沽酒》的题文："李白上街走，提壶去买酒，遇店加一倍，见花喝一斗，三遇店和花，喝光壶中酒，借问此壶中，原有多少酒？"

解法一：方程。

设，壶中原有 x 斗酒。

一遇店和花后，壶中酒为：$2x - 1$；

二遇店和花后，壶中酒为：$2(2x - 1) - 1$；

三遇店和花后，壶中酒为：$2[2(2x - 1) - 1] - 1$；

因此，有关系式：$2[2(2x - 1) - 1] - 1 = 0$；

解得：$x = 7/8$ 斗。

解法二：算术法。

逆推理得：

最后遇花喝一斗前：0+1=1；

最后遇店加一倍，则原有：1÷2=1/2；

第二次遇花喝一斗，原有：1/2+1=3/2；

第二次遇店加一倍，则原有：3/2÷2=3/4；

第一次遇花喝一斗，原有：3/4+1=7/4；

第一次遇店加一倍，则原有：7/4÷2=7/8

综合以上得：7/8 斗。

"古来圣贤皆寂寞，惟有饮者留其名。"李白所作词赋，宋人已有传记，就其开创意义及艺术成就而言，"李白词"享有极为崇高的地位。世人称之为"酒星魂""酒圣""酒仙"。古往今来，大概再没有别的哪个文人与酒的关系之密切和嗜酒的名气之大，能和李白相提并论。

李白是一位天才诗人，又是一位卓尔不群的酒仙。和李白同时代的伟大诗人杜甫有一首吟咏酒中八仙的诗，其中写道："李白斗酒诗百篇，长安市上酒家眠。天子呼来不上船，自称臣是酒中仙。"因此，李白"酒仙"的称号由此而来。

如此说来，李白又是从何时开始饮酒的呢？这还是需要李白自己来为大家解答。

李白有一首诗叫《答湖州迦叶司马问白是何人》：

"青莲居士谪仙人，酒肆藏名三十春。

湖州司马何须问？金粟如来是后身。"

诗中明确表示自己酒中仙人的名气很大，并且已有30年的酒龄。根据李白行踪考证，此诗大约写于至德元年（756年）。由此推算，李白的酒龄当从他二十四五岁开始。现存李白诗文1 000余篇，其中以酒、酌、饮、杯、樽、觞为题入诗的有200余首，约占全部作品的四分之一，但他早期的作品，即25岁以前，尚没有一首与酒有关。由此可见，酒仙李白也非生来便是嗜酒之人，也是后期慢慢培养出来的。

再说说李白的诗酒生活。25岁的李白仗剑出蜀，辞亲远游，开始了"酒隐安陆，蹉跎十年"的生活。李白在湖北安陆白兆山生活了10年，李白真正的诗酒生活是从安陆开始的。他来安陆不久，因遇故人，兴奋之下，开怀畅饮，以致第二天早晨头昏目眩，误把远处走过来的安州长史李京之当成好友魏洽，打马前趋，竟闯了李长史的道。

由于李白此时"若浮云而无依"，尚未"妻以许氏"，没有婚后那样的相门社会地位做后盾，于是写了《上安州李长史书》给李长史，以谢"闯道"之罪。文中写道："昨遇故人，饮以狂药。一酌一笑，陶然乐酣。困河朔之清觞，饮中山之醇酎。属早日初眩，晨霾未收，乏离朱之明，昧王戎之视。青白其眼，誊而前行，亦何异抗庄公之轮，怒螗蜋之臂？御者趋召，明其是非。入门鞠躬，精魄飞散。"

现代文译文：我要说的是，有个客居汝海的朋友，近日来到本地，昨天与他邂逅，开怀痛饮，你来我往，相互劝酒，不知不觉就喝得大醉。仍然是又吃又喝，无法投箸。一直到来日早晨，仍是昏昏沉沉。已经没了离朱那样心明眼亮的视力，更没有了五戎敢于直视太阳的眼力。两眼半睁半闭，懵懵懂懂趔趔趄趄向前走。和庄子说的没什么两样，举着两手，如螳螂怒臂而挡车辙。多亏为您驾车的那个人大声喊着跑过来，告诉我是怎么回事。走进君侯您的门来，酒才醒了大半，惊得魂飞魄散。

李白还有几首著名诗酒代表作。如《将进酒》：
"君不见，黄河之水天上来，奔流到海不复回。
君不见，高堂明镜悲白发，朝如青丝暮成雪！
人生得意须尽欢，莫使金樽空对月。
天生我材必有用，千金散尽还复来。
烹羊宰牛且为乐，会须一饮三百杯。
岑夫子，丹丘生，将进酒，杯莫停。
与君歌一曲，请君为我倾耳听。
钟鼓馔玉不足贵，但愿长醉不复醒。
古来圣贤皆寂寞，惟有饮者留其名。
陈王昔时宴平乐，斗酒十千恣欢谑。
五花马、千金裘，呼儿将出换美酒，与尔同销万古愁！"

这首诗大约创作于天宝十一年（752年），距诗人被唐玄宗"赐金放还"已达8年之久。当时，他跟岑勋曾多次应邀到嵩山（在今河南登封市境内）元丹丘家里做客。本诗反映作者才华横溢而又放荡不羁，因怀才不遇，乃诗酒自适。李白又有赠内诗，是诗人和妻子许夫人的戏谑之作。"三百六十日，日日醉如泥。虽为李白妇，何异太常妻。"

在李白流传于世的大量诗篇中，"赠内诗"所占的分量并不多，只有10余首。但即便是这为数不多的10余首诗，还是可以从中看到李白对妻子的一片深情。此诗以调侃之笔，活用东汉太常卿周泽一年"三百五十九日斋""一日不斋醉如泥"之典，自嘲醉酒之甚，戏谑安慰许氏夫人，幽默风趣，同时暗遣愁情。

李白漫游江夏、襄阳等地，创作了许多饮酒诗。李白在安陆10年，实际上是以安陆为中心漫游的10年，他曾东游淮扬，西入秦海，南抵朱陵，北越白水，足迹遍及大半个中国。在居长安期间，太子宾客贺知章闻其名，相会于紫极宫，称他为"谪仙人"，解金龟换酒，与之成为莫逆之交，造就了中国文坛的一段佳话。

在长安期间，李白同贺知章、李适之、汝阳王李琎、崔宗之、苏晋、张旭、焦遂等人被称为"酒中八仙"，杜甫有《饮中八仙歌》：

"知章骑马似乘船，眼花落井水底眠。

汝阳三斗始朝天，道逢麴车口流涎，恨不移封向酒泉。

左相日兴费万钱，饮如长鲸吸百川，衔杯乐圣称世贤。

宗之潇洒美少年，举觞白眼望青天，皎如玉树临风前。

苏晋长斋绣佛前，醉中往往爱逃禅。

李白斗酒诗百篇，长安市上酒家眠。天子呼来不上船，自言臣是酒中仙。

张旭三杯草圣传，脱帽露顶王公前，挥毫落纸如云烟。

焦遂五斗方卓然，高谈阔论惊四筵。"

《饮中八仙歌》是一首别具一格、富有特色的"肖像诗"。八个酒仙是同时代的人，又都在长安生活过，在嗜酒、豪放、旷达这些方面彼此相似。诗人以洗练的语言，人物速写的笔法，将他们写进一首诗里，构成一幅栩栩如生的群像图。

李白在游历江夏、襄阳等地之后，结识了韩朝宗、孟浩然等著名人物，留下了许多脍炙人口的诗篇。"山公醉酒时，酩酊高阳下。头上白接篱，倒著还骑马。"诗中将酒醉后的形态写得惟妙惟肖，如果李白不是常饮常醉，绝对写不出这种流传千古的醉酒诗。

只要翻翻李白的诗集，就不难发现他的生活中，几乎无处不有酒。正如郭沫若说的："李白真可以说是生于酒而死于酒。"关于他的死，还有种种不同的传说，大概都与饮酒有关。其中最富于浪漫主义情调的是说他醉后到采石矶的江中捉月亮时失足落水而死。虽然有些悲切，但是与酒仙一生放荡不羁的无拘自由生活倒也贴切。

李白者，恐怕也真真是这前无古人、后无来者之士，他留下来的诗作，以及种种的关于饮酒的事件，直至数百年后，仍将是脍炙人口的一段佳话。

14 Li Bai and Wine

In ancient times, most poets and writers liked drinking wine and they created tremendous eternal legends after drinking. For example, Wang Xizhi composed *Preface to the Poems Collected from the Orchid Pavilion*, gaining a great fame, Zhang Xu stunned people with his cursive, and Li Bai wrote hundreds of poems.

Li Bai is not only a poetic genius but also a "Wine Immortal". Once there was a poem about *Li Bai Buying Wine*: "Li Bai walked on a street, bringing a flagon to buy wine. Once stepping into a wine shop, he would fill it with more wine; once seeing flowers, he would drink one dou (ancient unit of weight, about 6.25 kg). After seeing shops and flowers for three times, he would drink all the wine in his flagon. How much wine is there in this flagon?"

Solution one: equation.

Assumption, there is x dou of wine in this flagon.

After Li Bai sees shops and flowers for the first time, the wine in this flagon is: $2x-1$;

Flowers for the second time, the wine in this flagon is: $2(2x-1)-1$;

Flowers for the third time, the wine in this flagon is: $2[2(2x-1)-1]-1$;

Therefore, a correlation is obtained: $2[2(2x-1)-1]-1=0$;

Conclusion: $x=7/8$ dou

Solution two: a mathematical approach.

Inference,

Before Li Bai sees flowers and drinks one dou for the last time, the wine in the flagon is: $0+1=1$;

Before Li Bai sees shops and adds wine for the last time, the wine in the flagon is: $1 \div 2=1/2$;

Before Li Bai drinks one dou when seeing flowers for the second time, the wine in the flagon is: 1/2+1=3/2;

Before Li Bai adds wine when seeing shops for the second time, the wine in the flagon is: 3/2÷2=3/4;

Before Li Bai drinks one dou when seeing flowers for the first time, the wine in the flagon is: 3/4+1=7/4;

Before Li Bai adds wine when seeing shops for the first time, the wine in the flagon is: 7/4÷2=7/8

Conclusion: 7/8 dou.

"How many great men were forgotten through the ages? But great drinkers are more famous than sober sages." Li Bai's poems were recorded by people of the Song Dynasty. In terms of their creative meanings and artistic achievements, "Li Bai's Poems" enjoyed a great reputation. Common people call him "soul of wine", "wine sage" and "wine immortal". From ancient to modern times, no one could be paralleled with Li Bai in terms of his relation with wine and his reputation for drinking wine.

Li Bai is a genius poet and a distinguished wine immortal. A poem about eight immortals of wine, written by Du Fu, a great poet lived in the same time as Li Bai, reads: "After drinking wine for one dou, Li Bai could write hundreds of poems and often slept in taverns in Chang'an Street. However, Li Bai refused to get on a boat even at the request of the emperor, and called himself immortal of wine." Therefore, Li Bai earned his name of "Wine Immortal".

So when did Li Bai start to drink wine? Li Bai himself will tell you in a poem named *Answer to Who is Li Bai for Buddhist Sima in Huzhou*:

"Demoted immortal of Buddhist Qinglian,
Having sheltered myself in taverns for more than thirty years.
Why you bother to ask me?
We both are Buddhist incarnations of Gold Millet Buddha."

This poem has clearly manifested that Li Bai enjoyed a great reputation as a wine immortal for 30 years of drinking. According to the research about Li Bai's whereabouts, this poem was written in about the first year of Zhi De (756 A.D.). Accordingly, we could safely draw a conclusion that Li Bai started to drink at the age of 24 or 25. There are about 1,000 poems by Li Bai, of which about 200 are on "wine, sip, drink, cup, wine goblet and wine cup". However, in his early works created before he was 25, no poem was found to be associated with wine. Thus it can be seen that Li Bai, a wine immortal, was not born a winebibber but gradually took a fancy for wine.

Here is another story about Li Bai's life of wine and poems. At 25, when he left Shu with a sword and began his life of "Settling down in Anlu drinking wine, killing time there idling away for ten years", his life of wine and poems really began. Shortly after arriving in Anlu, he met his old friends and drank so heartily out of excitement that he felt faint and dizzy even the next morning. Even worse, he mistook Li Jingzhi, the General Secretary of Anzhou, for his good friend Wei Qia, so he rode horse and went forward to meet him, unexpectedly, getting in the way of General Secretary Li.

At that time, Li Bai looked like "idle clouds without anything to rely on" without any post-marriage social status to back up him, so he offered an apology for his "obstructing the way" by writing *A Letter to General Secretary Li in Anlu*, which said: "I came across a friend yesterday. Out of excitement, we both drank so heartily until we became unconsciously drunk. However, we continued drinking until the next morning when we felt faint and dizzy without good eyesight like Li Zhu or Wang Rong, who dare to stare at the sun. With my eyes half-opened, I managed to stagger forward. Like what Zhuangzi said, holding my hands up, I looked like an angry mantis trying to stop a chariot. Thanks to your driver's yelling and running to me, I suddenly realised what was going on. I didn't wake up until walking near your chariot and being frightened half to death."

There are several famous masterpieces of Li Bai including *Invitation to Wine*:

"Do you not see the Yellow River come from the sky,

Rushing into the sea and ne'er come back?

Do you not see the mirrors bright in chambers high,

Grieve o'er your snow-white hair though once it was silk-black?

When hopes are won, oh! Drink your fill in high delight,

And never leave your wine-cup empty in moonlight,

Heaven has made us talents, we're not made in vain.

A thousand gold coins spent, more will turn up again.

Kill a cow, cook a sheep and let us merry be,

And drink three hundred cupfuls of wine in high glee!

Dear friends of mine,

Cheer up, cheer up!

I invite you to wine.

Do not put down your cup!

I will sing you a song, please hear,

O hear! Lend me a willing ear!

What difference will rare and costly dishes make?

I only want to get drunk and never to wake.

How many great men were forgotten through the ages?

But great drinkers are more famous than sober sages.

The Prince of Poets feast'd in his palace at will,

Drank wine at ten thousand a cask and laughed his fill.

A host should not complain of money his is short,

To drink with you I will sell things of any sort.

My fur coat worth a thousand coins of gold,

And my flower-dappled horse may be sold,

To buy good wine that we may drown the woe age-old."

This poem was written in about the 11th year of Tian Bao (752 A.D.), 8 years after Li Bai was demoted by Emperor Xu Zong of the Tang Dynasty. At that time, he and Cen Xun were often invited to Yuan Danqiu's home in Mount Song (in present Dengfeng, Henan province). This poem reflects that Li Bai is a talented and unconstrained person who lived a carefree life drinking and writing every day since he had no chance to realise his ideals. He also composed some poems for his wife, which are playful and teasing in nature. Here is one example, "Throughout the year, I got drunk every day. Although you are my wife, you have no difference from the wife of Tai Chang."

Among those poems spread in the world, there are ten "poems to wife", which just account for a minor part. However, we could still see Li Bai's deep love for his wife. This poem, in a teasing style, creatively applied the story of Tai Chang Qin Zhou Ze in the Eastern Han Dynasty, who fasted for 359 days but got drunk on one day. Li Bai used this self-mockery to console his wife Xu, showing his great humour and sorrow.

During the decade in Anlu, Li Bai traveled extensively. He went eastward to Huaiyang, westward to Qin Sea, southward to Zhuling and northward to Baishui, making his footprints in most areas of China. When he was staying in Chang'an, Li Bai met He Zhizhang, a guest of prince, in Ziji Palace and was given the name "Demoted Immortal". He Zhizhang used his own accessories to exchange wine, and finally became a confidant of Li Bai, which made a much-told story on everybody's lips in Chinese literary world.

During his stay in Chang'an, Li Bai, together with He Zhizhang, Li Shizhi, Li Jin (the King of Ru Yang), Cui Zongzhi, Su Jin, Zhang Xu, Jiao Sui, were known as "The Eight Immortals of Wine". Du Fu wrote a poem named *Eight Immortal Drinkers*:

"After drinking wine, he rode a horse like rowing a boat, vacillating and staggering. Dazzling, he fell down into a well and slept there.

Not until had he drunk for three dou did Li Jin go to meet the emperor. On his way to the palace, he met a carriage which was full of distiller's yeasts, making his mouth watering. He regretted that he could not move to another place like Jiuquan county, which has many vineries.

Out of interest, he spent thousands of Liang (silver) on wine every day. He drank just as a whale swallows water. He claimed he drank freely in order to abandon politics.

He, a handsome youth, always turned his nose to the sky when raising his glass and drinking. His posture was so decent and gentle.

Although he is a vegetarian before Buddha, he often totally forgot all the commandments while drinking.

After drinking wine for one dou, he could write hundreds of poems. He often slept in inns while drinking on Chang'an Street. The emperor held a party beside lakes, and asked Li Bai to make a preface for a poem. However, he refused to get on a boat because he drank too much, and called himself 'wine immortal'.

After drinking three cups, he could readily write calligraphy, and he was called 'cursive sage' by people living at the time. He did not stick at trifles, and he even took off his hat before Wang Xizhi. His writing was as fluent as clouds spreading on paper.

He would feel drunk and refreshed with cups of wine, and his talk would always electrify his listeners."

Eight Immortal Drinkers is a "portrait poem" with a distinctive style. The eight immortals of wine all lived in the same era. They also lived in Chang'an and had many similarities including drinking wine, and bearing bold and unconstrained characters. Using concise words and a sketch method, Du Fu put all of them in one poem, presenting a vivid and lively image of the group.

Traveling around Jiangxia, Xiangyang, and other places, Li Bai made friends with Han Chaozong, Meng Haoran and other celebrities, leaving us many popular poems. "Every time when Shan Jian got drunk, he would stagger in Pool Gao Yang. Wearing his white kerchief, he rode home sitting backward." This poem vividly depicts the image of a drunkard. If Li Bai were not such a person, he would not have written such poems which have spread through the ages.

When you leaf through the *Selected Poems of Li Bai*, you will find that "drinking wine" is a major topic. Just like Guo Moruo said: "Li Bai was born and died for wine." There are many legends about his death. In general, all are linked to wine drinking. Among them, the most romantic story is about his death after drinking. It held that Li Bai went to Caishiji River to catch the moon after drinking, but unfortunately slipped and fell into water. Although it is a sad story, it is in accordance with Li Bai's unconventional and unrestrained life style as a "wine immortal".

Li Bai, perhaps is a person without parallel in history. The poems he left and the many tales about his drinking remain much-loved stories today.

15 李白黄鹤楼搁笔的故事

历代文人歌咏黄鹤楼的诗篇，最著名的当数唐朝崔颢那首七律《黄鹤楼》。因为有了这首诗，诗仙李白也不得不感叹"眼前有景道不得"，所以，在《李太白全集》中，我们是找不到登临黄鹤楼的诗篇的。李白倒是写过"捶碎黄鹤楼"的诗句，为此还引起了一场小风波。

在黄鹤楼公园东边，有一亭名为"搁笔亭"，亭名取自"崔颢题诗，李白搁笔"的一段佳话。唐代诗人崔颢登上黄鹤楼赏景写下了一首千古流传的名作：

"昔人已乘黄鹤去，此地空余黄鹤楼。

黄鹤一去不复返，白云千载空悠悠。

晴川历历汉阳树，芳草萋萋鹦鹉洲。

日暮乡关何处是，烟波江上使人愁。"

后来李白也登上黄鹤楼，放眼楚天，胸襟开阔，诗兴大发，正要提笔写诗时，却见崔颢的诗，大为折服说："一拳捶碎黄鹤楼，一脚踢翻鹦鹉洲。眼前有景道不得，崔颢题诗在上头。"便搁笔不写了。这个传说或出于后人附会，未必真有其事。

李白虽因服气崔颢作品而搁笔，未写出登黄鹤楼的诗，但他心中总觉若有所失。他眺望江心的鹦鹉洲，心生一念：我何不效学崔颢，也作一首这种格调的诗呢？于是，题为《鹦鹉洲》的七律就这样诞生了：

"鹦鹉来过吴江水，江上洲传鹦鹉名。

鹦鹉西飞陇山去，芳洲之树何青青。

烟开兰叶香风暖，岸夹桃花锦浪生。

迁客此时徒极目，长洲孤月向谁明？"

诗前四句与崔诗如出一辙。但这样的诗，显然还无法与《黄鹤楼》相比。直到他到了金陵，登上凤凰台，面对滔滔东流的长江水，有感于六朝的兴废和国运的衰落，才触发灵感，写出一首气象格律皆堪与《黄鹤楼》相匹敌的《登金陵凤凰台》：

"凤凰台上凤凰游，凤去台空江自流。

吴宫花草埋幽径，晋代衣冠成古丘。

三山半落青天外，一水中分白鹭洲。

总为浮云能蔽日，长安不见使人愁。"

这首诗与《黄鹤楼》都称得上是盛唐七律佳作，但因崔作在前，李白拟作在后，后人议论纷纷，崔颢和《黄鹤楼》的名气也就被越抬越高。

759年，李白在流放夜郎（在今贵州省）的途中遇赦返回，到江夏时遇到当时任南陵（在今安徽省）县令的故人韦冰，两人对饮叙旧。诗人有满腹心事，于是即席写下了著名的长篇政治抒情诗《江夏赠南陵韦冰》。诗中的"我且为君捶碎黄鹤楼，君亦为吾倒却鹦鹉洲"二句，简直匪夷所思，李白也因此被视为狂人，有些人还写诗文来讥笑他。有个少年丁十八讥笑李白："黄鹤楼依然无恙，你是捶不碎的。"为此，李白又写了《醉后答丁十八以诗讥予捶碎黄鹤楼》一诗：

"黄鹤高楼已捶碎，黄鹤仙人无所依。

黄鹤上天诉玉帝，却放黄鹤江南归。

神明太守再雕饰，新图粉壁还芳菲。

一州笑我为狂客，少年往往来相讥。

君平帘下谁家子？云是辽东丁令威。

作诗调我惊逸兴，白云绕笔窗前飞。

待取明朝酒醒罢，与君烂漫寻春晖。"

在这首诗中，李白用诙谐的笔调向丁十八"赔罪"：你怪我惊动你的"逸兴"，作诗问罪，可是黄鹤楼已经被我捶碎，黄鹤仙人也无处栖止了。好在黄鹤可以上天向玉帝诉苦，玉帝会放黄鹤归来，黄鹤楼也会重建起来的。至于我，只有等酒醒了再来陪你同游。

虽有人不信此诗是李白所作，但李白"捶碎黄鹤楼"的故事却已不胫而走。

实际上，李白热爱黄鹤楼到了无以复加的程度，他高亢激昂，连呼"一忝青云客，三登黄鹤楼"。山川人文，相互倚重，崔颢题诗，李白搁笔，从此黄鹤楼之名更加显赫。黄鹤楼则沾了这两位诗人的光，成为中国四大古典名楼之一。

15 Li Bai Lays Down His Pen at the Yellow Crane Tower

History witnessed many famous poems about the Yellow Crane Tower, written by different poets. The most renowned one is *The Yellow Crane Tower*, a seven-character octave, written by Cui Hao who lived during the Tang Dynasty. Because of this poem, even the Immortal Poet Li Bai had to confess: "Even though I saw such splendid views, I could not write them down in a poem." Thus, in *Anthology of Li Bai*, we cannot find any poem about his ascending the Yellow Crane Tower. Nevertheless, he wrote a verse "smash the Yellow Crane Tower", triggering another incident in history.

At the east side of the park of Yellow Crane Tower stands a pavilion named "Pavilion of Laying down the Pen", which comes from a story between Cui Hao and Li Bai. Cui Hao ascended the Yellow Crane Tower to enjoy sceneries, and created a masterpiece spreading through all the ages:

"The stage on yellow crane was gone amid clouds white.
To what avail is Yellow Crane Tower left here?
Once gone, the yellow crane will ne'er on earth alight;
Only white clouds still float in vain from year to year.
By sunlit river trees can be count'd one by one;
On Parrot Islet sweet green grass grows fast and thick.
Where is native land beyond the setting sun?
The mist-veiled waves of River Han make me homesick."

Afterwards, Li Bai also mounted the Yellow Crane Tower. Inspired by the splendid views, he was excited to write a poem. The moment he saw the poem written by Cui Hao, he was so impressed by the superb poem and said: "I want to smash the Yellow Crane Tower, and kick down the Parrot Shoal. I could not restrain myself from writing poems, but Cui Hao's poem compelled me to lay down my pen." Then he laid down his pen with a sigh. However, it may be a rumour, instead of a true story.

Although he was convinced by Cui Hao's poem, and laid down his pen without writing a poem about the Yellow Crane Tower, he still felt disoriented. When he saw the Parrot Shoal located in the centre of the river, he thought to himself: why not make a poem in a similar rhythm to Cui Hao? Then, he wrote a seven-character octave titled *The Parrot Shoal*:

"The miraculous parrot ever came to Wujiang River,
Leaving a legend of eternal life.
Today, the parrot flew away and back to Mount Long,
Leaving the shoal in verdant trees and grasses.
The fragrant atmosphere of orchid is full of excitement,
And peach blossom fell to the river and aroused water wave.

I, a banished man, could only see Chang'an in the distance in vain,

Who can truly see the bright and true face of the moon over the shoal?

Above the shoal, for whom the moonlight shone?"

The first four lines are similar to Cui Hao's poem, but certainly, this poem is still inferior to *The Yellow Crane Tower*. Not until he arrived at Jinling and ascended the Phoenix Terrace, seeing the Yangtze River flowing east, and recalling the ups and downs and the decline of the Six Dynasties, did he write down a poem *On Phoenix Terrace at Jinling*, which was comparable to *The Yellow Crane Tower* in image and rhythm:

"On Phoenix Terrace once phoenixes came to sing,

The birds are gone but still roll on the river's waves.

The ruined palace's buried 'neath the weeds in spring;

The ancient sages in caps and gowns all lie in graves,

The three-peak'd mountain is half lost in azure sky;

The two-fork'd stream by Egret Isle is kept apart.

As floating clouds can veil the bright sun from the eye,

Imperial Court now out of sight saddens my heart."

This poem and *The Yellow Crane Tower* are both regarded as masterpieces of seven-character octave poetry in the glorious age of the Tang Dynasty. But because Cui Hao wrote his poem before Li Bai, doubts and comments that Li Bai's poem is an imitation never stop. As a result, Cui Hao and his poem have a stronger reputation.

Li Bai was banished to Yelang (in present Guizhou province) until an amnesty declared in 759 A.D. by Emperor Suzong Qianyuan. On the way back, he met his old friend Wei Bing in Jiangxia, who was the county magistrate of Nanling County (in present Anhui province). They drank and talked about the old days together. Full of concerns and worries, Li Bai wrote the famous political and lyric long poetry *To Nanling Wei Bing in Jiangxia*. The verse "I smashed the Yellow

Crane Tower for you, and you turned over the Parrot Shoal for me too." was so incredible that many readers thought Li Bai was a maniac. Some people even wrote articles and poems to laugh at him. A youth named Ding Shiba ridiculed him: "The Yellow Crane Tower still stood there steadfastly, and you could not smash it!" In reply, Li Bai wrote a poem named *In Response to Ding Shiba's Ridicule in Drunk*:

"I have smashed the Yellow Crane Tower,

Making immortals no home.

Cranes flew to tell the Jade Emperor,

Who let them back home.

Prefecture chief had it rebuilt and redecorated,

Making the pink walls still smelling.

People made fun of me for being crazy,

Even you, a young fellow could ridicule me.

I found Yan Junping and asked him about you,

He told me your ancestor was Ding Lingwei who served in Liaodong

You wrote the poem to make fun of me,

For ruining your mood for poem.

You want to stay until tomorrow when I sober up,

I will let accompany you to enjoy the romantic spring."

Li Bai used witty words to make an apology to Ding in this poem. He said: "You Ding Shiba, wrote a poem to blame me for ruining your poetic mood with my poem. But the Yellow Crane Tower has already been smashed by me, and immortals living in the tower have become homeless now. Fortunately, yellow cranes could fly into the sky to find the Jade Emperor and accuse me. And he would let cranes come back and the tower could be rebuilt well. As for me, we can go out together in spring after I sober up."

Even though some people doubted that this poem was written by Li Bai, this story spread far and wide.

In fact, Li Bai loved the tower so deeply that he even yelled with passion and excitement: "I was shamed of being your visitor, who has ascended the Yellow Crane Tower three times." Because of this story, the tower, with both natural and cultural reputation, enjoys a greater fame. Thanks to the two brilliant poets, it has become one of the four renowned towers in China.

16 李白金陵"跳月"的故事

南京夫子庙前，有一座文德桥。听老辈人说，每逢冬月十五月亮当头的时候，站在桥头朝水上看，倒映在水里的月影子刚好分成两半：桥这边半个，桥那边半个。

圆圆的月亮影子，为什么会分成两半呢？这里有段故事。

传说唐朝大诗人李白，有一次到金陵（今南京）来，在文德桥旁边的一座酒楼上歇脚。这天碰巧是冬月十五，到了晚上，他就独自坐在酒楼上赏月，一边喝酒，一边吟诗作赋。李白生平最喜爱月亮，说月亮又干净又好看。这天晚上，他抬头看见天上的月亮洁白滚圆，心里非常高兴，就多喝了几杯。到了半夜，李白趁着酒兴，下楼走到文德桥上。他刚走上桥，一低头，忽然看见月亮掉在水里了，河水一动，洁白的月影上就添了几条黑纹。李白这时喝得醉醺醺的，只当是月亮给河水弄脏了。他靴子也顾不得脱，张开双手就跳下桥去捞月亮。谁知这一跳，月亮没捞着，却把水里的月亮震破了，顿时分成了两半儿。

这个传说故事就这样传下来了。后来人们在文德桥旁边修了个"得月台"，据说那里就是当年大诗人李白赏月的地方。

16 Li Bai "Jumps into the Moon" in Jinling

In front of the Confucius Temple in Nanjing stands the Wen De Bridge. According to what the older generation say, on the fifteenth day of every winter month when the full moon hangs above in the sky, the shadow of the moon reflected in the water happens to be halved by the bridge.

Why did the round shadow of the moon fall into two halves?

A legend held that Li Bai happened to come to Jinling (present Nanjing) on the fifteenth day of that winter month and took a rest in an inn beside Wen De Bridge. When evening came, he sat alone in the inn enjoying the full moon, chanting poems over drinking. Li Bai liked the moon most in his lifetime because it is clear and beautiful. That night, looking up at the round and bright moon, Li Bai got excited and drank a lot. At midnight, out of excitement of drinking, Li Bai went downstairs and came to Wen De Bridge. Once stepping on the bridge and lowering his head, he saw the moon falling down into the river and stirring the water, which wrinkled the pure moon shadow with alternate white and black. Li Bai got drunk at that time, and thought the moon was stained by the water. Forgetting his boots, he stretched his arms and jumped into the water to fish for the moon. Nobody would have thought that the moon was split into two halves.

This tale came down generation after generation. The later generation built a "Platform of Catching the Moon" beside Wen De Bridge, where the great poet Li Bai appreciated the moon in those years.

17 李白与"骗子"汪伦的故事

李白在漫游生涯中曾受过骗，但他不仅不生气，反而与"骗子"结为好朋友，这个"骗子"就是汪伦。

桃花潭，在安徽省南部青弋江的上游（今泾县境内），是个风景幽美的地方。这里一直流传着一个感人的故事。唐朝时，桃花潭边有个叫汪伦的青年人，因家贫读书不多，但很爱听诗书，每次下田经过村头的私塾，见老先生讲诗书，总是悄悄地在窗边听一会儿。当时，诗人李白已名扬天下，汪伦很喜爱他的诗，他常常想：要是能亲眼见到李先生，该多么幸福啊！

有一年春天，李白从宣城的敬亭山到泾县城边的水西。当时，水西是风景优美的胜地：翠竹亭亭掩古塔，泉水潺潺绕寺前。李白在此玩赏了数日，作了不少诗，流连忘返。李白到水西的事不知怎么被汪伦知道了，他立刻驾一叶小舟，顺着青弋江的碧波来到了水西，一路打听，找到了李白。施礼拜见后，李白问这布衣打扮、素不相识的俊俏后生找自己有什么事，汪伦又鞠躬说："我叫汪伦。听说先生喜欢饮酒吟诗，今特来奉告，有一个好去处，不知先生可愿前往？"他指着闪闪发光的青弋江说："我就住在这条江的上游，那里有一个桃花潭，岸上有十里桃花、万家酒店。"李白一听开心极了，"哇！十里桃花，那该有多美！万家酒店，我可以尝到多少美酒啊！"李白越想越高兴，欣然应邀前往。

到了桃花潭边，但见潭水悠悠，野渡舟横。岸上只有一树桃花，孤零零地开着，桃花树边，有一个茅店，门前屋檐下，一根细竹竿斜挑着一面杏黄色的酒旗，在春风中哗啦啦地飘舞。

"你骗我，"李白不悦，"哪里有什么'十里桃花，万家酒店'？"汪伦笑道："不瞒先生说，我们刚才经过的地方，叫十里边山，这小店门前的那棵桃花，不是'十里桃花'吗？"汪伦又指着窗外那面迎风飞舞的酒旗说：

"喏，那不写得清清楚楚，是'万家酒店'嘛，酒店主人姓万。"李白一听，这才发现自己上了汪伦的"当"！李白也笑了，连连点头："好一个'十里桃花''万家酒店'，原来如此，骗得巧妙！"李白并不以为被愚弄，反而被汪伦的盛情和机智所感动。

汪伦将李白请进小酒店，布置了简单的酒菜，这才把心底话儿全掏了出来："先生，我是个山野鲁莽之人，平时很喜欢你的诗，也很想见你一面。这次听说你到了水西，一心想请先生到寒舍做客，又怕先生嫌我们家贫，不肯光临，因此想了这么个主意。晚生欺骗了先生，请先生宽恕！"说罢，纳头便拜。

李白被汪伦的一片真心实意感动了，他双手扶起汪伦，深情地说："你要早说明，我也会来的。我很喜欢你，我俩交个朋友吧。"汪伦激动地拉住李白的手，热泪滴落在李白的衣袖上……

就这样，李白在桃花潭住了十多日，受到汪伦和村人的热情款待。李白每天饮酒、赏景、阔论，流连数日后才登舟去庐山。李白临走那天，汪伦恋恋不舍，带着全村的人一起在岸上踏步唱歌为他送行。李白感动得眼泪都流出来了，他诗兴大发，脱口一首绝句《赠汪伦》：

"李白乘舟将欲行，忽闻岸上踏歌声。

桃花潭水深千尺，不及汪伦送我情。"

这首诗因为情真意切、情景交融，成为歌颂友谊和送别的经典之作被千年传诵，汪伦亦因李白的诗句名扬天下，名垂青史。

17 Li Bai and "Liar" Wang Lun

During his roaming life, Li Bai was "tricked" several times. But he was not angry with the "liars", and made friends with them instead. Wang Lun was one of them.

The Peach Blossom Lake, located in the upstream of Qingyijiang River in southern Anhui province (in present Jing county), was a scenic place. A heart-warming story happened there which has been passed on from generation to generation. Beside the lake lived a young man, Wang Lun, who could not receive much education because of his poor family. But he was so fond of reading that he would quietly listen to the tutor for a while outside the classroom window every time he passed the private school on his way to farm work. At that time, Li Bai was already very famous, so Wang Lun loved his poems so much so that he always thought to himself: it would be great if I were to meet Li Bai!

One spring, Li Bai traveled around from Mount Jingting in Xuancheng to Shuixi which at that time was a famous scenic place with an ancient pagoda shrouded by green bamboos, and a temple close to a babbling spring. Li Bai stayed there for several days and wrote quite a few poems. Afterwards, Wang Lun heard about Li Bai's arrival and immediately rowed to Shuixi. Finally, he met Li Bai with the help of local people. Wang Lun bowed before Li Bai and said: "Sir, my name is Wang Lun. I heard that you love wine and poems, so I came here to see whether you would like to go to a great place for fun." He pointed to the sparkling Qingyijiang River and said: "I lived upstream of this river, by the side of which the Peach Blossom Lake is located. Around the lake, a blossoming peach garden extends ten *li* (pronounced as "shili" in Chinese) and there are ten thousand (pronounced "wanjia" in Chinese) wine shops there." Hearing this, Li Bai felt so excited and thought that he could appreciate peach blossom and drink nectar to his heart's content! Therefore, he said yes and readily went there with great expectations.

However, when he arrived at the lake, what he saw was quiet lake water, docked boats on shore, and only one peach tree in blossom alone on the lake bank. Next to the tree was a thatched house with an apricot wine flag plucked on a thin bamboo pole, fluttering in the breeze.

Li Bai was unhappy and blamed Wang Lun: "You lied to me!" Wang Lun smiled and replied: "Dear sir, actually, the place we just passed by was named

Mount Shili (ten *li*). And here is this peach tree, so we could call it 'shili peach blossom', right?" Then he pointed to the fluttering wine flag and said: "You see, this inn is named Wanjia (ten thousand) Shop, because Wan is the family name of its owner." After hearing this, Li Bai found out he was "tricked" by Wang Lun. He laughed and said: "I see, so that is what it is, you are so smart!" Li Bai was not angry, on the contrary, he was so moved by Wang Lun's wit and hospitality.

Wang Lun invited Li Bai to go to the inn and ordered simple meals. Then, he told Li Bai the truth: "Sir, I am just a vulgar farmer who loves your poems deeply and want to meet you desperately. When I heard about your arrival in Shuixi, I really wanted to invite you to my humble home, but I feared that you would not be willing to come to my poor home. So I had to come up with this idea. I am so sorry that I lied to you and I do beg your pardon." Wang Lun bowed his head to the ground again for Li Bai's forgiveness.

Moved by Wang Lun's sincerity, Li Bai held up Wang Lun's two hands and said with deep emotion: "If you had told me the truth, I would also have come here with you gladly. I like you, so why not make friends with each other?" Wang Lun was so thrilled, holding Li Bai's hands tightly with tears dropping on Li Bai's sleeve.

Li Bai stayed there for more than ten days, and was warmly treated by Wang Lun and other hospitable villagers. Everyday, he drank good wine, enjoyed terrific views and talked with others. Several days later he set out to Mount Lu. Wang Lun was reluctant to bid farewell to Li Bai, so he sang farewell songs for Li Bai with other villagers. Li Bai was moved to tears. Then he could not constrain himself but sang an extemporaneous *jueju* titled *To Wang Lun Who Comes to Bid Me Farewell*:

"I, Li Bai, sit aboard a ship about to go,
When suddenly on shore your farewell songs overflow.
However deep the Lake of Peach Blossoms may be,

It's not so deep, O Wang Lun, as your love for me."

The blending of sincere feeling and natural settings makes this poem a classic and widespread one praising friendship and bidding farewell. Also, thanks to Li Bai's poem, Wang Lun become famous in ancient Chinese history.

18 李白沉香亭畔醉填《清平调》的故事

唐玄宗非常欣赏李白的诗才，召李白进京，任命他为翰林学士。这时的唐玄宗已由励精图治的英明君主，变成了骄奢淫逸、只图享乐的皇帝，整天贪恋酒色，不务朝政。他召李白进京，只是想利用李白的诗章，为他自己歌功颂德、粉饰太平，增加宫廷生活的乐趣，并不想让李白参与朝政。

李白虽任翰林学士，但只是一个虚衔，并无实权。尽管李白的诗才得到了唐玄宗的欣赏，但由于政治抱负得不到施展，他的满腔热血、一片肝胆无处倾诉，一身才智无所用处，因此常常闷闷不乐，借酒消愁。

一天，正当李白独自在宫廷外一处酒楼上闷闷饮酒的时候，唐玄宗和杨贵妃正在宫中对酒赏花，连夜欢筵。因为这一天是杨贵妃的生日，唐玄宗便命梨园供奉李龟年等人请李白进宫将今天赏心乐事写成诗歌，以为永久纪念。

李龟年一行数人找遍了翰林院所有角落，也没有见到李白的影子，便亲自带人到闹市上的所有酒家查寻。他们找了几个酒店，还是没有见到李白的影子，着急之际，忽然听到一家酒楼上有人引吭高歌：

"三杯通大道，一斗合自然。

但得酒中趣，勿为醒者传。"

李龟年一听就知道是李白的声音，急忙奔到楼上去请。谁知李白已烂醉如泥，在酒桌上睡着了。李龟年无奈，只好差人将李白扶下楼去，用马将他驮到金銮殿。

玄宗见李白醉成这个样子，急忙令人在自己身边给李白铺了一块毯子，并叫贴身宫女口含清水给李白喷面。

不多时，李白渐渐醒来，当他看清在自己身旁坐的是玄宗皇帝和杨贵妃时，不禁大吃一惊，急忙起身跪下请罪。

唐玄宗不仅没有怪罪他，反而让人端来已准备好的醒酒汤。玄宗亲自给他调温，赐给他喝下。李白喝了醒酒汤，神志清醒多了，只见眼前一片火红、粉红、紫、黄和雪白的木芍药花，在皎洁的月光和灯火照耀下，争奇斗艳，栩栩飘香。玄宗皇帝见李白已清醒了，便对李白说："贤卿，今日是贵妃的生日，又正好赶上牡丹盛开，我和贵妃前来观赏，朕特召你作首新词，以助雅兴。"

李白谢过万岁，命人拿起笔来，抬头看了看争奇斗艳的牡丹花，又看了看含情脉脉、满脸红晕的杨贵妃，便乘酒后的余兴，铺纸挥笔，一口气写了三首著名的《清平调》：

"云想衣裳花想容，春风拂槛露华浓。
若非群玉山头见，会向瑶台月下逢。

一枝红艳露凝香，云雨巫山枉断肠。
借问汉宫谁得似，可怜飞燕倚新妆。

名花倾国两相欢，常得君王带笑看。
解释春风无限恨，沉香亭北倚栏杆。"

这三首诗，把牡丹和杨贵妃交互在一起写，花即人，人即花，人面花光浑融一片，同蒙帝恩。从结构上看，第一首从空间写，引入月宫阆苑。第二首从时间写，引入楚襄王阳台，汉成帝宫廷。第三首归到现实，点明唐宫中的沉香亭北。以第一首春风与第三首春风，遥相呼应。

第一首第一句，见了云便想起贵妃的霓裳羽衣，见了牡丹花便想起贵妃玉容。下句露华浓，进一步点染牡丹花在晶莹的露水中显得分外娇艳，使花容人面更见精神。下两句想象升腾到天上的群玉山、瑶台、月宫等仙人世界，这些景色只有天上才见，实把杨贵妃比作天女下凡。

第二首指出楚襄王为梦中神女断肠，那及眼前的绝代佳人。再说汉成帝的皇后赵飞燕，还得倚仗新妆，那里及得眼前花容月貌的杨贵妃，无须脂粉，全是天然绝色。这儿以压低神女和赵飞燕来抬高杨贵妃。

第三首一、二句把牡丹、杨贵妃、玄宗三位融合为一体。倾国美人当指杨贵妃，第三句中"春风"二字即君王之代称。

唐玄宗对此诗很满意，后人编造说，高力士因李白命其脱靴，认为受辱，乃向杨贵妃进谗，说李白以飞燕之瘦，讥杨贵妃之肥，以飞燕之私通赤凤，讥杨贵妃之宫闱不检，这是不可靠的。

李白写完，李龟年立即将李白写好的新词献给唐玄宗。唐玄宗将新词置于御案，从头至尾细细读了一遍。他见李白醉中写出的新词仍然笔墨酣畅、文采盎然、隽永别致，不禁高兴地用手拍着御案，点头连称："好，好，好啊，爱妃诞辰喜日，贤卿为朕写出这样绝妙好诗来，足以光灿千古了！日月不能掩其精华，流年不能减其光彩。"说完，忙将新词转给杨贵妃，贵妃接过新词，见字字喷珠涌玉，笔笔牵心动人，读着读着心都要醉了。她欣喜不禁地将新词交给梨园供奉李龟年，命他立即率乐工、歌伎，在筵席前演唱。

李龟年率众歌伎在欢快的《清平调》旋律中，唱起了李白为杨贵妃写的新词。在欢快的音调中，杨贵妃心花怒放，禁不住迈开轻盈的脚步，在花前月下飞舞起来。半醉了的唐玄宗，痴痴地望着杨贵妃的舞姿，也高兴地让身边宫女取来一支玉笛，随着《清平调》乐曲的节拍，兴致勃勃地吹了起来。

杨贵妃舞完一曲，端起七宝盏，亲自斟上一杯西域酿造的葡萄酒，赏给李白。李白谢过贵妃，双手接过这杯美酒，一饮而尽，不久便昏昏然地沉睡过去了。

18 Li Bai Drunkenly Writes *The Beautiful Lady Yang* at Chenxiang Pavilion

Emperor Xuanzong, who deeply appreciated the poetic talent of Li Bai, summoned him to the capital and appointed him to serve the Imperial Academy. However, he was not an industrious and ambitious emperor any more but an extravagant emperor who was addicted to wine and women. Consequently, he had no energy to govern the country. He summoned Li Bai to the capital to write poems to sing his accomplishments and morality and to bring fun to the life in the palace. Therefore, in no way could he give chance to Li Bai to participate in political affairs.

Although Li Bai was an imperial poet, he was given a nominal official title without any real power. Although his poetic talent was appreciated by the emperor, he could not realise his political ambitions. Although he was full of enthusiasm for politics, he found nowhere to release it. Therefore, he became depressed and indulged himself in wine to drown his sorrows.

One day, while the emperor and the beautiful Lady Yang was drinking and appreciating flowers overnight in their palace, Li Bai drank alone in a pub outside the palace. That day was Yang's birthday, so the emperor ordered Li Guinian to send for Li Bai to the imperial court and asked him to write a poem to in memory of the magnificent event.

Li Guinian and several others searched every part of the Academy but could not find Li Bai. Then they went out searching all pubs in the downtown, trying to find him. Li Bai was so anxious when he suddenly heard someone singing loudly:

"Cups of wine can lead us to the right way,
  Casks of wine corresponds to the nature.

I only want to get the delight of wine,
  The delight is hard to tell by sober people."

Once hearing this voice, Li Guinian recognized that it was Li Bai. So he hurriedly ran upstairs only to find him drunk and sleeping at the table. Li Guinian had no choice but to ask his attendants to hold Li Bai downstairs and put him on a horse, and finally took him to the Throne Hall.

Seeing Li Bai so drunk, Emperor Xuanzong immediately asked his servants to put a blanket by the side of him and help Li Bai lie down. Meanwhile, he asked his personal maid to use her mouth to spray water on Li Bai's face to wake him up.

After a while, Li Bai slowly woke up and was totally shocked when he found the emperor and Lady Yang sitting next to him. Then he got down on his knees in a hurry to apologise humbly to the emperor.

Fortunately, the emperor did not blame him but asked a servant to serve him with warm soup, which helped him wake up quickly. After finishing the soup, he sobered up and saw the peony blossoming in flaming red, pink, purple, yellow and white. Those flowers competed with each other for beauty and fragrance in the bright moonlight and candle flame, giving off a pleasing flavour. Seeing Li Bai sobered up, the emperor said: "My dear minister, today is my dearest Yang's birthday and coincidentally peony is in full bloom these days. So we came here to enjoy flowers. I specially called for you and hope you could write a new poem to entertain us."

Li Bai thanked the emperor for appreciation and asked a servant to bring him a writing brush. He raised his head, looking at the colourful flowers and lovingly blushed Lady Yang and then, in a drunken excitement, he wrote three famous stanzas of *The Beautiful Lady Yang*:

  "Her robe is made of cloud, her face of flowers made,
  Caressed by vernal breeze, freshened by morning dew,

Charming as Fairy Queen in her Mountain of Jade,
Or Goddess of the Moon in her palace sky-blue.

A branch of peony with her fragrance impearled,
Sweeter than Mountain Goddess bringing showers in dreams,
Unrivalled by the beauties of the ancient world,
Not even by Flying Swallow in her dress that gleams.

The beauty gazes at the flower she admires,
Winning the monarch's smiling gaze from hour to hour.
Gratifying spring wind's insatiable desires,
She leans on balustrade north of the Fragrant Bower."

These three stanzas bring the flower and Lady Yang together, one resembling the other. The face of Yang and the colour of flowers integrated and both enjoyed the imperial favour. From a structural point of view, the first stanza describes the moon and the palace where immortals lived. From the time perspective, the second stanza depicts the court of King Xiang of Chu State and Emperor Cheng of the Han Dynasty. The last stanza describes the reality and the north of the Fragrant Bower. "Vernal breeze" from the first line and "spring wind" from the last line obviously echo with each other.

The poem's opening line implies that once he saw clouds, he immediately thought of Lady Yang's rainbow-colored and beautiful dress; and that once he saw the flowers of peony, he immediately thought of Lady Yang's pretty face. In the second line, "freshened by morning dew" further emphasizes the beauty of the peony flowers with crystal morning dew, revealing the beautiful appearance of flowers and Lady Yang. In the last two lines we see more depictions of abodes for immortals, like Mountain of Jade and the palace at the moon where Fairy Queen lived. Thus a celestial atmosphere was created in this terrestrial poem. Actually it praised fairy-like Lady Yang who came from the paradise.

The second stanza mentions the Goddess of Witch Mountain who made the King Xiang of Chu State heartbroken and Zhao Feiyan, the queen of Emperor Cheng of the Han Dynasty, needed makeup. Both beauties are far behind Lady Yang who is naturally beautiful. Here, Li Bai praised Lady Yang by belittling the Fairy and Zhao Feiyan.

The first and the second lines in the last stanza integrated the three essential parts: peony, Lady Yang and the emperor. Certainly, the beauty is Lady Yang, and the "spring wind" is a symbol of the emperor.

Emperor Xuanzong was very satisfied with this poem. Later people made up such a story that Gao Lishi, a powerful eunuch, was insulted by Li Bai who asked him to take off his own boots; so Gao Lishi told Lady Yang that Li Bai was satirized her who was so plump by contrasting Zhao Feiyan, who was so slim and had some affairs with a man named Chifeng. Certainly this story is not true.

After Li Bai finished this new poem, Li Guinian immediately handed it to the emperor. The emperor placed the poem on the imperial table and read it thoroughly from beginning to end. Even after getting drunk, Li Bai still wrote an elegant and unusual poem with fluency and literary grace. The emperor was so excited and couldn't help slapping the imperial table to speak highly of Li Bai's poem: "Great! Great! On my dearest Lady Yang's birthday, you wrote such a brilliant and wonderful poem for me, it must be a masterpiece with eternal fame. The sun and the moon cannot mask its essence, and the time cannot eliminate its brilliance." Then, he passed the poem to Lady Yang at once. After reading the poem, she also thought that every word in it was delicate like precious jade and jewelry, every character was touching and moving. Out of her excitement, she gave the poem to Li Guinian, a theatrical performer, and commanded him to lead some instrumentalists and singing girls to perform before the feast began.

Then, Li Guinian led some singing girls to sing this poem in a cheerful tune. Hearing this lively melody, Lady Yang was wild with joy and couldn't help dancing at a graceful and light pace. The emperor, in a semi-drunk state, gazing at

Yang's graceful dance affectionately, ordered a maid to bring a jade flute for him and played it to the rhythm of the poem.

When the dance came to an end, Lady Yang held the Qibao cup and poured precious wine for Li Bai in person. Li Bai took it thankfully with his both hands, and drank it off. Soon he was fast asleep.

19 李白醉写番书的故事

忽然有一天,有一个来自渤海国的番使带着国书到达长安,朝廷派贺知章迎接安排番使。

第二天,番使送给朝廷国书一封。唐玄宗宣召翰林学士,打开番书,竟然一个字也不认识,都跪在地上说道:"这封信都是些鸟兽文字,我们学识浅薄,不认识一个字。"玄宗就叫杨国忠看看,杨国忠打开一看,两只眼睛就像瞎了一样,也是一个字不认识。玄宗就宣诏文武百官,但还是没有人认识一个字,更无法知道信上写的是什么了。玄宗非常气愤,大骂这些无用大臣:"你们这些文武百官,竟然没有一个是饱学之人,谁也不能为国家分忧解难。这封信认不出来,怎么回话,怎么能让番使回去?让他们耻笑我大唐王朝,以为我大唐王朝无人,他们必定会侵犯我边界,这可怎么办?限令3天,如果没有人能知道番书的意思,一律停薪;6天之内,如果还没有人能知道,一律撤职;如果9天还不能知道番书的内容,一律处斩。再选其他的大臣,保护大唐江山。"

圣旨一下,文武百官都默默无语,再也没有一个人敢讲话。玄宗更加烦恼。

贺知章回到家里,把这些事一五一十都讲给李白听了。李白微微冷笑说:"可惜我李某去年没有考中,不能给天子分忧解难了。"贺知章大吃一惊,连忙问道:"你博学多识,一定能认识番书,我一定在皇上面前保举你。"

第二天，贺知章就向玄宗汇报说："我家有一个秀才，叫李白，博学多识，要想认识番书，非他莫属。"玄宗非常高兴，立即派遣大臣，带着皇帝的诏书到贺知章家，要李白奉诏上殿。

李白对宣诏大臣说道："我李白乃是一个微不足道的普通百姓，无才无识，朝廷里有很多官僚，都是博学之人，为什么要向我这样的人请教，我不敢奉诏，生怕得罪朝廷显贵。"

大臣把这事向玄宗禀奏。玄宗又向贺知章说道："李白不肯奉诏，他到底是什么意思？"贺知章回答说："我知道李白文章盖世，学问渊博。只因为去年在考场中，被主考官屈批了卷子，轰出门去，今天叫他以一个普通人的身份朝拜天子，心里有愧。请皇上赐给他一个名位，再派一个大臣去，一定会奉诏来的。"玄宗说道："同意你的意见。赐李白进士及第，可以穿紫袍金带。就麻烦你去迎接李白，你一定不要推辞。"

贺知章领了圣旨，回到家中，请李白去阅读番书，把玄宗求贤若渴的心情一一说给李白听。

李白身穿御赐紫袍金带，就骑马随着贺知章一起入朝。唐玄宗正在等着李白的到来，一见李白，如贫得宝，如暗得灯，如饥得食，连忙说道："现在有一封番信，没有人能读懂，所以特此宣诏你来，希望你能为社稷分忧。"李白谢恩，躬身说道："我因为学识浅薄，被太师批了一个不取，高太尉把我轰出考场。我是被批无用的秀才，不能令主考官满意，怎么能使皇上满意呢？"玄宗说道："我非常了解你，请你不要推辞。"就叫侍臣把番信捧出来给李白看。李白看了一遍，微微冷笑，当着文武百官的面，把番信用流利的长安话翻译出来。其实，那封信也很简单，无非是警告玄宗皇帝不要再侵犯它，并要玄宗将高丽割让的176个城池给它，如果不答应，就兴兵讨伐。

文武百官听完李白朗读的番书，大惊失色，面面相觑。唐玄宗听了，更是神情不悦，愁云满面。沉思了很长时间，才向文武百官问道："现在番兵要抢占高丽，有什么好的办法可以拒敌？"文武百官，就像泥塑也似的没有人敢回话。

贺知章启奏说："太宗皇帝三次征伐高丽，不知死伤多少人马，消耗多少财物，也没有取胜。幸好盖苏文死了，盖苏文的几个儿子为争权夺利互相残杀，给了我们可乘之机，高宗皇帝派李斌、薛仁贵统帅百万大军，这才消灭高丽，使他们归顺。现在天下太平，多年不遇战事，既没有良将也没有精兵，如果打起仗来，很难说能不能取胜。兵连祸结，不知要到什么时候才能安宁，愿皇帝明鉴。"

玄宗问道："我们该怎样回答番使？"贺知章说道："皇上可以问问李白，他必定善于辞令。"玄宗于是就召见李白，问如何回复的事，李白说："皇上尽管放心，不必多虑。明天召见番使，我当面回答他，也用鸟兽一般文字。言语中一定羞辱番家，一定要他们的可毒知我大唐王朝的威严，拱手来降。"玄宗问道："谁是可毒？"李白奏道："渤海这个地方的风俗，称他们的大王叫可毒，就好像回纥族人称他们的大王叫可汗，吐鲁番叫赞普，六诏叫诏，诃陵称悉莫一样，都是各地的不同风俗。"玄宗见李白应对自如，滔滔不绝，当天就封李白为翰林学士，设宴款待李白，李白也无所顾忌，尽量而饮，直到喝醉为止。

第二天早朝，李白醉酒未醒，被内官催促着进朝。百官朝见完了，玄宗召见李白上殿，只见李白脸上酒气未退，两只眼睛还显得蒙蒙眬眬。玄宗叫御厨弄三份醒酒酸鱼汤来，亲自给李白调汤。李白跪着喝下汤去，顿时觉得神清气爽。当时百官见皇帝器重李白，又惊又喜，唯有杨国忠、高力士心里极为不舒服，表现出轻蔑来。不一会儿，玄宗召见番使，李白紫衣纱帽，飘飘然就像神仙驾临人间一样，双手捧着番信，站在左边的大柱子下，朗读起番信来，只读得铿锵悦耳，一字不差。番使极为吃惊，心想：不知从哪里来的高人，竟如此精通我国文字。正惊异间，李白朗声说道："小小番国，竟敢如此无礼，蔑视我大唐王朝。皇上圣明，宽大为怀，不与小人计较。现在皇上有诏在此，请番使仔细听好。"番国使臣战战兢兢，跪在阶下。玄宗叫在御座旁边安置七宝床，准备好阗白玉砚，象管兔毫毛笔，独草龙香墨汁，五色金花信笺。吩咐李白到御座前，坐在锦墩上写诏书。

李白奏道："我的靴子不干净，恐怕弄脏了席，请皇上开恩，赐臣脱靴解袜上去。"玄宗同意了，叫一个小内侍替李白脱靴子。李白又说道："我有一句话，乞求皇上赦臣狂妄，我才敢说。"玄宗说道："随便你说，我不会怪罪你。"李白这才整了整衣服，说道："我前次考试，被杨太师批了个不中，又被高太尉赶出考场。今天看见他们两个人都在，我的精神不足，恳望皇上吩咐杨国忠太师替我捧砚磨墨，高力士太尉替我脱靴解袜。只有这样，我才能精神抖擞，提笔写诏，一挥而就，才能保证完成皇上吩咐的任务。"玄宗觉得这事也有点过分，但用人之际不好多说，只好传旨，叫杨国忠捧砚，高力士脱靴。杨国忠、高力士心里非常清楚，这是李白依仗皇帝的宠幸，报复他们两人，出于无奈，不敢违背皇上，敢怒不敢言，只好遵旨。

19 Li Bai Drunkenly Answers a Credential

One day, an envoy of Bohai Kingdom came to Chang'an with a credential. He Zhizhang was assigned to meet and entertain him.

The next day, the envoy presented a diplomatic credential to the imperial court. Emperor Xuanzong summoned the Hanlin Academicians to meet him and read the credential. But, none of them could understand and explain it. They knelt on the ground and responded: "We couldn't understand it because it was written in special characters which are beyond our limited knowledge." Then, Emperor Xuanzong required Yang Guozhong to have a look. He was shocked and stood there as though he were blind, because he recognized no word. Finally, Emperor Xuanzong summoned all the officials and asked them to recognise it, yet no one could. Emperor Xuanzong was very angry, and scolded those useless officials: "You are the officials to protect our country, but none of you is learned. Now, nobody can shoulder the responsibility and share my cares and burdens. What shall we do to respond to the credential and send the envoy back? More importantly, others will laugh at us for lack of talents, and they will certainly violate our borders. I will give you guys three days to figure out its meaning, otherwise, your salary will be suspended; if nobody can do it in six days, all of you will be dismissed; if no one can do it in 9 days, all of you will be executed. And then, I will select other officials who could take the responsibility to protect our country."

After the imperial edict came, all of the officials remained silent and no one dared to speak to the emperor, which made Emperor Xuanzong more annoyed.

He Zhizhang told Li Bai everything about the matter. With a slight sneer, Li Bai said: "It is a pity that I failed the exam, so I have no opportunity to share the worries of His Majesty." Hearing this, He Zhizhang was very surprised and said to Li Bai: "I know you are such a knowledgeable person that you can definitely recognise the credential. I will recommend you to the emperor tomorrow."

The next day, He Zhizhang reported to the emperor: "Li Bai is a scholar who lives in my home. He is a knowledgeable man and can understand these special characters." Emperor Xuanzong was very pleased and sent one minister with the edict to He Zhizhang's home, and asked Li Bai to go to the imperial court.

Li Bai said to the minister: "I'm just an ordinary insignificant person without talent or knowledge. There are many bureaucrats who are all learned, why ask me for help? I'm really afraid of offending those officials, so I can't obey the emperor's summons."

The minister told this to the emperor. Emperor Xuanzong asked He Zhizhang: "What did he mean by saying so?" He Zhizhang answered: "Li Bai is knowledgeable and his articles are matched by no one. Due to a mistake of the examiner in correcting his paper last year, he was turned down. Now, he felt ashamed as an ordinary person to serve His Majesty. Please give him a position, and send one minister to invite him. I'm sure he will come." "You are right. Now, as a scholar, he can wear an official suit. And can you take the trouble to invite him?"

Afterwards, He Zhizhang took the edict and went back home. He invited Li Bai to recognise the credential by telling him how desperate Emperor Xuanzong was for talents.

Li Bai wore official suits and rode on horse to the imperial court with He

Zhizhang. Emperor Xuanzong was eagerly waiting for Li Bai who was a source of hope for him. Seeing Li Bai, the emperor immediately said: "Here is the credential, but no one can recognise it and understand its accurate meaning. So I invite you to come over and hope you can share my concern." Li Bai expressed his thanks to the emperor and said with a bow: "Because of my limited knowledge, I wasn't accepted by the prime minister and even was expelled from the examination room. As a loser, I wasn't recognized by the examiner, so how can I satisfy His Majesty?" Emperor Xuanzong answered: "I know you very well, please do not refuse my request." Then, the emperor asked his courtier to show the credential to Li Bai. Li Bai glanced at it with a sneer, and translated it fluently in Chang'an dialect at the presence of all officials. In fact, the credential was very easy, warning Emperor Xuanzong not to invade the territory of Bohai Kingdom, and to cede 176 cities from Goryeo. If the emperor refused the request, a war would be launched against him.

Learning all about the credential, the officials present looked at each other in speechless despair and turned pale with fright. Emperor Xuanzong was even more annoyed and full of sorrow. Thinking for a moment, the emperor asked those officials: "Now, the soldiers of the Bohai Kingdom will invade Goryeo, have you got any idea about it?" Those officials were stunned and had no reply.

He Zhizhang responded: "Emperor Taizong attacked Goryeo three times, but finally failed. The other consequences were human loss and property destruction. Fortunately, Gaesomun died, and his sons fought each other for power and benefits. Then Emperor Gaozong seized the chance and sent a million strong army led by Li Bing and Xue Rengui to attack Goryeo, and eventually conquered them. Now, we have been living in a peaceful world without war for years. So we have neither excellent generals nor good soldiers. If we started a war, the consequence of it would be more uncertain. The war disasters would happen for successive years and no one knows when it would stop. So may His Majesty consider it carefully."

"How could we answer the envoy?" Xuanzong asked. "You can ask Li Bai, he is very wise." He Zhizhang answered. Then, Xuanzong summoned Li Bai and asked him how to respond to the envoy. Li Bai said: "Take it easy. When you summon the envoy tomorrow, I will answer him in their language. I will humiliate him and let Kedu know the power of our country. Finally, they will surrender to us." Xuanzong asked: "Who is Kedu?" "This is the custom of Bohai Kingdom, they called their king Kedu, as Uyghur people called their king Kehan, Tubo people called Zanpu, Liuzhao people called Zhao, the Heling people called Ximo, it is just the custom of different countries and nationalities." Xuanzong was very satisfied with the answer of Li Bai, and appointed him as a Hanlin Scholar. The emperor also hosted a banquet in honour of Li Bai. Li Bai felt at ease and drank until he was drunk.

The next day, Li Bai was still sleepy from drunkenness when he was hustled to the imperial court. After the officials' meeting with the emperor, Li Bai was summoned to meet him. Seeing Li Bai walking in a drunken and drowsy way, the emperor asked the royal chef to bring three bowls of sour fish soup to make him recover more quickly, and he seasoned the soup for Li Bai in person. After drinking the soup, Li Bai felt refreshed. All the officials were surprised at the benefits Li Bai had received except Yang Guozhong and Gao Lishi who showed disdain. After a while, when the envoy was summoned to meet Xuanzong, Li Bai appeared like a fairy with official suits. Li Bai stood by the left pillar holding the credential with both of his hands and reading it aloud without any mistakes. The envoy was very surprised at the strange expert who was good at their language. Suddenly, Li Bai said loudly: "How dare that one small country could despise our country in this disrespectful way. But luckily, our wise emperor is broad-minded, so he doesn't want to argue with anyone. Here is an imperial edict, please listen carefully!" Then, the envoy gingerly kneeled on the floor. Xuanzong asked his courtier to place a seat beside his throne and prepared a jade inkstone, a rabbit fur brush, scented ink and special stationery. And then, he invited Li Bai to be seated and write the imperial edict.

Li Bai said: "I'm afraid my dirty boots would stain the seat, so I hope you will allow me to take off my boots." Xuanzong nodded and asked one courtier to help him. But Li Bai added: "I beg you forgive my impoliteness." Xuanzong said: "Speak out what you want, I won't blame you." Then Li Bai adjusted his clothes and said: "In the last exam, my paper was denied by Grand Preceptor Yang, and I also was expelled from the examination room by Grand Commandant Gao Lishi. They are here today, so I can't concentrate my mind. I beg you to order Grand Preceptor Yang Guozhong to hold the inkstone and Grand Commandant Gao Lishi to take off the boots for me. Only then can I concentrate on writing the imperial edict successfully." Although Xuanzong was not in favour of his request, he knew that Li Bai was irreplaceable. Finally, he accepted Li Bai's request. Yang Guozhong and Gao Lishi knew Li Bai's purpose, but they couldn't refuse the emperor, so they obeyed His Majesty's order.

20 李白蔑视权贵的故事

唐玄宗叫李白当了翰林学士，是个没什么实权的官。所以，李白辅助皇上治理国家的理想仍然不能实现。

当时，朝廷大权把持在宰相李林甫和宦官高力士等人手里。一些想升官发财的人，都变着法儿巴结他们。李白却打心眼里蔑视他们。

这天，李白心中烦闷，来到酒楼喝酒，喝得七八分醉了，忽然，宫中的梨园长（歌舞班子的负责人）李龟年跑进来说："李学士，皇上召你立刻进宫！"

原来，唐玄宗同杨贵妃在宫中的沉香亭里观赏牡丹花，叫李龟年率领一群梨园子弟唱歌助兴。他们唱的是老词，唐玄宗听腻了，想起李白会作诗，就派人来叫他去写新歌词。李白听了，满不在乎地说："几首歌词算什么！来，喝几杯再去！"

"不行不行！皇上和贵妃娘娘已经等候半天了！"李龟年急得满脸通红。

"皇上？我……我李白可是酒中仙人呐，我……我酒还没喝够哩！哈哈哈……"李白大笑着说。

李龟年看李白醉了，不由分说，命令同来的人架起李白就往外走。来到沉香亭，李白酒还没醒。唐玄宗见了李白这个样子，倒也没怪罪他，让人给李白喝了醒酒汤，扶他躺在了床上。

据说这时候，李白已经清醒了。他见高力士正在身边，想起他平时作威作福的样子，有意要杀杀他的威风。

"脱靴！"李白装作醉醺醺的神态，突然把脚朝高力士一伸。

高力士一听，差点气歪了鼻子，正要发火，看见皇帝朝自己连连递眼色，只得忍气吞声地替李白脱下了靴子。

过了一会儿，李白爬起身来，向唐玄宗行礼请罪。唐玄宗没有生气，只是叫李白马上写出三章《清平调》的新歌词来。

李白想了一会儿，很快就写好了。李龟年谱上曲，演唱起来。唐玄宗亲自在一旁吹笛子伴奏。杨贵妃陶醉在悠扬动听的乐曲声中，高兴得眉飞色舞。从此，唐玄宗就更加器重李白了。

可是，一帮权贵却恨死了李白。他们造谣诽谤，故意中伤李白。高力士还挑唆杨贵妃在唐玄宗跟前说李白的坏话。唐玄宗听信了他们的话，渐渐疏远了李白。

李白目睹朝廷如此腐败，也不愿在这儿再待下去，就上了一份奏章，请求辞去翰林学士的职务。唐玄宗立刻批准了。李白身穿锦袍，骑着五花马，一会儿高声歌唱，一会儿纵情大笑，出了长安城门。

后来，李白在很多诗里都写了他宁愿过穷困生活，也不愿去巴结权贵的志气。如"安能摧眉折腰事权贵，使我不得开心颜！"

20 Li Bai Despises Bigwigs

Li Bai was appointed by Emperor Xuanzong to be a Hanlin Scholar with no real power. So his political ideal of assisting the emperor in governing the country could not be realised.

At that time, prime minister Li Linfu and eunuch Gao Lishi held the political power. Those who wanted to be promoted tried hard to please them in various ways. However, Li Bai really despised them.

One day Li Bai was in a bad mood and went to a pub. He was already half-drunk when Li Guinian, the director of the opera team, ran to the pub and said to Li Bai: "Scholar Li, His Majesty has summoned you to the palace!"

In fact, Emperor Xuanzong and Lady Yang were enjoying peony flowers with Li Guinian and his opera actors were performing for fun. But Emperor Xuanzong was tired of hearing those stale songs, so His Majesty invited Li Bai, who was famous for his poetry, to write new songs. Having received the request, Li Bai said carelessly: "It is merely several songs, you needn't worry about it. Bring me more wine."

"No, His Majesty and Lady Yang have waited for you for a long time!" said Li Guinian anxiously.

"The emperor? I am wine immortal, I haven't had enough! haha..." Li Bai laughed.

Seeing Li Bai in a drunken state, Li Guinian ordered some attendants to remove Li Bai from the pub. But Li Bai was still drunk when they came to the Chenxiang Pavilion. Emperor Xuanzong didn't blame him, but asked servants to bring some soup for him to sober up and helped him to lie in bed.

It was said that at that moment Li Bai already sobered up. But he was unhappy about being awoken from his drunkenness by Gao Lishi, so he wanted to play a trick on him.

"Take them off!" drunken Li Bai stretched his foot in front of Gao Lishi.

Hearing this, Gao Lishi was so angry at Li Bai's action that he was about to lose his temper when he received hints from the emperor. So he had to suppress his fury and restrain himself to take off Li Bai's boots.

After a while, Li Bai stood up and apologized to Emperor Xuanzong. But Emperor Xuanzong wasn't angry, and he just asked Li Bai to compose three chapters of *The Beautiful Lady Yang*.

Li Bai thought for a moment and then completed the song quickly. Then Li Guinian composed a tune and sang it. At the same time, Emperor Xuanzong accompanied him on the flute. Lady Yang felt very happy and was intoxicated by the music. Hence, Li Bai won more trust from the emperor for his talent.

But a band of bigwigs hated Li Bai so much, so that they slandered him on purpose with all kinds of rumours. Gao Lishi persuaded Lady Yang to say something bad about Li Bai in front of Emperor Xuanzong, who believed what they said and gradually drifted away from Li Bai.

Despairing over corruption at the imperial court, Li Bai presented a letter resigning from his post. After getting the immediate approval of Emperor Xuanzong, Li Bai put on his robe, rode his horse, and left Chang'an, laughing and singing.

In many of his later works, Li Bai expressed his ambition that he would rather live a poor life than associate with those bigwigs, which can be easily evidenced in the following verse: "How can I stoop and bow before the men in power, and so deny myself a happy hour?"

21 "铁杆粉丝"追星李白三千里的故事

追星一族,自古已有,唐代的魏万,就是慕名追寻李白数千里的奇人。"大唐文坛第一明星"李白被朝廷变相地赶出京城以后,他原来所交的那些势利朋友马上就换了一副脸孔——不理大诗人了。然而,有个叫魏万的年轻人,却成了李白的"铁杆粉丝",十分仰慕他的天纵诗才,且不顾世俗的浊流,非常想结识这位名满天下的大诗人。

魏万(生卒待考),原名炎,后名颢,尝隐居王屋山,故号王屋山人,后在上元初登第。

年轻的魏万非常崇拜"诗仙"李白,于是在唐天宝三年(744年)仲春,他决定并立即出发,开始了他对李白疯狂的追寻。他从王屋山出发,日间行走,夜里则焚香沐手,抄录李白诗卷。并在住宿、吃饭、喝茶时都故意议论李白,以期打听到李白的行踪。魏万听说李白在哪儿,他就赶过去。可是魏万刚到,人家告诉他李白已经走了,真可谓是"一个后脚到,一个前脚走"。就这样,从黄河流域经几千里地,来到江南。又寻踪转会稽、下明州、奔天台、往永嘉、入缙云,还是追不上李白。魏万没有泄气,在畅游仙都后,又北上金华,……从江南又追寻回江北。直至翌年(745年)春,才与李白相遇于广陵,也算是皇天不负有心人吧!

魏万见到李白时,一身风尘,泪流满面,扑倒在地,双手捧上自己花了一年时间写成的48韵的《金陵酬李翰林谪仙子》,请李白指正。接着头也没抬,就叙述了一年多来追赶李白的艰辛以及沿途所见的风光。

李白感其情真意切的数千里相访,结合自己与魏万的共同游历,一气呵成了120韵长诗——《送王屋山人魏万还王屋》以赠别魏万。

在这首长诗中,写缙云风光的就有16韵。李白歌颂缙云风光16韵中的"岩开谢康乐",这"谢康乐"就是山水诗宗师谢灵运。于是,"岩径开从谢康乐,诗章著自李青莲"在缙云民间千百年来广泛流传。

在李白出了长安以后，魏万踏着诗人的游踪，马不停蹄，足足追了3 000里，才在广陵见到了李白。两人见面后，一同游赏自然风光，切磋诗歌艺术，谈得很投机，成了一对知心朋友。

魏万说："一长复一少，相看如兄弟。"

李白说："相逢乐无限！"

大诗人见魏万诚挚忠厚、年轻有为，特别高兴，因此对他非常信任，不仅托魏万照顾他的儿子，还把自己的全部诗稿交给魏万，让他印成集子。

不久以后魏万中了进士，他不负重托，编出了《李翰林集》，他是李白生前唯一一个为李白编诗文集的人，而且，他自己还饱含热情地写了一篇序。

魏万所编的李白诗集虽早已散佚，但他的这篇序却流传到了今天，而成为他们真诚友谊的见证。

21 A Die-Hard Fan Chases Li Bai for Three Thousand *Li*

Idolaters were not strange to the ancients, Wei Wan in the Tang Dynasty was a typical example, who chased Li Bai for thousands of *li*. When Li Bai was banished from the capital by the emperor, various snobby friends of his immediately danced to another tune and even they began to keep away from him. However, one young man named Wei Wan became a big fan of Li Bai. He admired the poetic talent of Li Bai and disregarded social conventions and desperately wanted to make friends with the popular poet.

Wei Wan (date of his birth and death are unknown), renamed as Yan, and then renamed as Hao, lived in seclusion in Mount Wangwu, which gave rise to the name "the person of Mount Wangwu". He succeeded in the imperial civil service examination at the beginning of the Shangyuan year.

Young Wei Wan worshiped the immortal poet Li Bai, so he decided to go after Li Bai during the mid-spring of the third year of Tianbao of the Tang Dynasty (744 A. D.). Starting from Mount Wangwu, he walked during the day and copied the poems of Li Bai in the evening after burning incense and washing his hands (a rite before a Buddhist copies the Buddhist scriptures to worship God). He deliberately talked about Li Bai during the time of accommodation, eating and drinking tea for getting some information about Li Bai. Wei Wan would go anywhere Li Bai stayed. However, many times Wei Wan was told that Li Bai had just left before he arrived. All the way from the Yellow River basin to Jiangnan, he traveled a few thousand *li*. Although Wei Wan chased Li Bai to Kuaiji, Mingzhou, Tiantai, Yongjia and Jinyun, he still did not catch up with him. Wei Wan wasn't discouraged, he continued to Jinhua after visiting Xiandu and went back to Jiangbei from Jiangnan. Until the following spring (745 A.D.), he met Li Bai in Guangling, which could be regarded as "God helps those who help themselves".

When Wei Wan met Li Bai, tired and with tears, he threw himself immediately to the ground and presented his 48-rhyme *Meeting Hanlin Li in Jinling* to Li Bai for correction, which was finished within one year. Then without raising his head, he described the hard experiences of chasing Li Bai and the scenery along the way.

Li Bai was so grateful to Wei Wan for his visit from a faraway place that he wrote a piece of 120-rhyme poem *Send Wei Wan back to Mount Wangwu*, which was related to their travels.

In this long poem, 16 lines are about the scenery in Mount Jinyun. In the line "Rocks are opened by Xie Kangle", Xie Kangle refers to the master of scenic poem Xie Lingyun. Consequently, the word "Mountain paths made by Xie Kangle while poems composed by Li Qinglian" has been widely known among folks in Mount Jinyun since then.

Since Li Bai left Chang'an, Wei Wan also began his journey to follow Li Bai. Finally, he met Li Bai in Guangling after chasing him for 3,000 *li*. Since then they became good friends, appreciating natural scenery and talking about poems together.

Wei Wan said: "An elderly and a youth play together, looking just like a pair of brothers."

Li Bai responded: "It's really a wonderful meeting!"

The great poet also appreciated Wei Wan's honesty, sincerity and ability, so he trusted him very much. He not only entrusted his son to Wei Wan but also asked him to have all his poems printed.

Soon after their meeting, Wei Wan succeeded in the imperial civil service examination and completed *The Collection of Hanlin Li*. He was the first and the only one who completed the collection of Li Bai during the poet's lifetime. He also wrote a passionate preface to it.

Although the collection of Li Bai completed by Wei Wan was scattered and lost, the preface has been widely circulated till today and has become a testament of their true friendship.

22 李白骑驴过华阴县衙的故事

据说，唐朝天宝年间，在长安供奉翰林的大诗人李白，政治上不受重视，而生活上又屡遭权贵们的逸毁。因而他对当时的统治集团，也就失掉了信心。于是，他就离开了京都长安，又开始了他那游山玩景的生涯。

李白离开长安城，骑了一头小毛驴，一颠一簸地向东走来。他很想攀上华山，观赏一下太华三峰的奇峻风光。一天，他来到华阴县境内，听人说华阴县令是个贪赃枉法的坏官吏，心想，一个小小的县令，也是如此的坏。他就记在了心上。

一天清晨，他打听到华阴县令正在衙门议事，就醉意蒙眬地倒骑着毛驴，来到县衙门口察看。李白的这一行动，被县衙的差役看见了，就把此事禀告给县令。县令一听，非常生气，厉声说道："何处狂士，竟如此放纵。"于是县令立即遣人，把李白的毛驴牵入县衙。李白来到县衙，跳下驴背，醉眼睨视了一下县令。县令一见，是个狂傲之士，遂厉声问道："你是何等之人？竟然这等无礼！"李白哈哈大笑一声，不慌不忙地说："无姓无名，曾用龙巾拭吐，御手调羹，力士脱靴，贵妃捧砚，天子殿前尚容我走马，华阴县里就不许骑驴！"

华阴县令一听，不禁吓得出了一身冷汗！他连忙走下堂来，跪倒在地上，磕头如捣蒜似的，回道："不知翰林至此，不知翰林至此，恕罪，恕罪！"李白瞟了县令一眼，说道："你身受国家爵禄，不能体恤黎民之苦，反而贪赃枉法，坑害百姓，罪恶多端。如果再不改邪归正，实难饶恕。"县令一听，连忙答道："小官记下了，小官记下了。"李白看到县令如此惊状，遂转过身走出县衙，又骑上驴背，向华山走去。

李白来到华山下，跳下驴背，走进山谷。那时华山的路，坎坷崎岖，草石绊径，有些地方还得攀藤附崖，实在难走。可是，这些困难却没有挡住他那欣赏太华三峰的雄心。他边走边看，时而欣赏一下华山的峻奇风光，时而寻访着仙洞胜迹，时而和深居于山林的隐居者促膝相谈，时而要求樵夫讲述华山的神话与传说。他走着，上着，听着，问着，终于登上了三峰，并在莲花峰顶上写下了《王真仙人歌》这首诗。

据说，李白登上最高的落雁峰巅后，心情激动极了。他望着重峦叠嶂的秦岭，眺着来自天际的黄河，不由得振衣高呼，"此处呼吸之气，恨不携谢眺惊人之句来！"

李白游完华山以后，又写下了《西岳云台歌送丹丘子》和《西上莲花山》等几首诗。

22 Li Bai Passes Huayin County *Yamen* Riding a Donkey

It is said that the great poet Li Bai who was appointed as Hanlin Scholar worked in Chang'an during the years of Tianbao of the Tang Dynasty. However, he was not only politically under-appreciated, but also often slandered by men of high ranks. Losing his confidence in the authorities, he left Chang'an and started traveling in various places.

He went eastward riding a little donkey when he left Chang'an. He really wanted to climb Huashan Mountain and enjoy the spectacular views of the three peaks. One day, he came to Huayin county, and heard that the county magistrate was a corrupt official. A county magistrate with little power was so bad, he thought. So he kept this in mind.

One morning, in a slightly tipsy state, Li Bai rode a donkey backward to the county *yamen* to have a look when he heard the county magistrate of Huayin was discussing official business there. However, his strange actions were seen through by the *yamen* runner who reported it to the county magistrate. The county magistrate was very angry and said harshly: "Who is he, how can he be so rampant?" Then he had Li Bai's donkey led along into the county *yamen*. Li Bai jumped down from the donkey and leered at the county magistrate in a drunken way. Seeing this arrogant man, the county magistrate asked angrily: "Who are you? How dare you are so rude!" Li Bai answered unhurriedly: "I am nobody, but I used the imperial towel to swipe away vomit. The emperor also seasoned soup for me in person. Gao Lishi took off boots for me and Lady Yang even held the inkstone for me. The emperor even permitted me to ride horse before the imperial court, can't you allow me to ride donkey here?"

Hearing this, the county magistrate was so frightened that he began to sweat. Then he hurriedly walked down his seat, kneeled on the ground and made a rapid succession of kowtow: "Sorry, I don't know you are here. Please forgive me, please!" Li Bai glanced at the county magistrate and said: "As an official, you are granted with government welfares. Instead of taking care of people, you take bribes and harm common people. If you don't mend your way, you will not be forgiven." The county magistrate hurriedly replied: "I will keep your words in mind." Seeing the county magistrate so frightened, Li Bai turned around and walked out of the county *yamen*. Riding his donkey, Li Bai went to Huashan Mountain.

The road to Huashan Mountain was full of jagged rocks and weeds and people even need to climb the cliff in some places. So it was really difficult for Li Bai to climb the mountain. But these difficulties couldn't prevent him from appreciating the three peaks of Huashan Mountain. Walking on the road, sometimes he enjoyed the spectacular views, sometimes visited the fairy caves, sometimes he had good talks with those hermits living in mountain forests and sometimes listened to legends about Huashan Mountain from the woodcutters. Finally, he topped the three peaks and wrote a poem titled *The Song of the Immortal Wang Zhen* at the Lotus Peak.

It was said that Li Bai was really excited when he topped the highest Wild Goose Peak. Looking at the Qinling Mountains with peaks rising one after another and the vast Yellow River, he shouted: "I can take a fresh breath here. I regret that I have not taken poet Xie Tiao's poetry here to chant."

After this traveling, Li Bai wrote several other poems including *Song about Yuntai of West Mountain—Farewell to Dan Qiuzi* and *Ascending the Lianhua of West Mountain*.

23 海上钓鳌客李白的故事

人类猎鱼垂钓始于何时，已无法确切考证，但垂钓由人类获取生存食物来源到把它当成融情寓志、陶冶情操却是一个不小的进步。3 000多年前的姜太公钓于渭水之滨的传说是人所共知的。姜子牙用直钩垂钓，钓鱼乎？钓志乎？寓志于钓罢了。

于是，垂钓成了历代文人志士融情寓志的一种手段。唐代自称"钓鳌客"的大诗人李白，便是其中之一。

李白是我国唐代的著名诗人，还是一位垂钓能手。李白的诗作有1 000多首，直接描写垂钓的或以垂钓作比兴写就的诗作多达四五十首。如"漾楫怕鸥惊，垂竿待鱼食"（《姑熟溪》），"闲来垂钓碧溪上，忽复乘舟梦日边"（《行路难·其一》）。

李白性情豪放不羁，对朋友，坦率真诚；对权贵，宁折不弯；对祖国大好山河，赞颂不已。这些品格、思想，在他的垂钓诗歌中都有反映。

古籍记载，李白年轻时在四川就常和诗友一起喝酒、吟诗、钓鱼、舞剑，并称此为"人生四大乐趣"。唐代著名现实主义诗人杜甫在评价李白时就说："诗卷长留天地间，钓竿欲拂珊瑚树。"可见，李白与垂钓结下了不解之缘。李白把垂钓同饮酒会友、吟诗纵情和舞剑抒怀视为四大乐事，足见他把自己的情感融入了垂钓之中。垂钓成了李白融情寓志的一种手段，反过来也成了他情感宣泄的一种方式，使他的"诗卷长留天地间"。

伟大的诗人李白，也曾去垂钓，不仅如此，在赵德麟《侯鲭录》卷六里记载了一个关于李白垂钓的故事。据说李白有一次上宰相府，封一版（送上一封信），上题曰："海上钓鳌客李白。"宰相笑问："先生临沧海钓巨鳌，以何物为钩线？"李白说："以明月为钩，虹霓为线。"宰相又问："用什么做钓饵呢？"李白高声道："就用天下最无义气的士大夫作钓饵。"宰相闻言不禁毛骨悚然。

在声名显赫的宰相面前，李白居然称自己是"钓鳌客"，足见他那壮志凌云的气概多么豪迈，让宰相都不由得吃了一惊。用彩虹做线，用月牙做钩，用无意气的士大夫为饵，在一望无际的东海巨浪中钓鳌，这该是何等的顶天立地！

李白以"钓鳌客"自喻，抒写了他要治国平天下的伟大抱负；把天下无意气的士大夫全都挂到钩上去钓鳌，何等气魄，何等痛快！大有以天下为己任的豪情。如果真的让李白执宰，天下无意气的士大夫全都被拿去钓鳌了，剩下的岂非一个清明坦荡的世界！

然而，可惜历史没有这样安排。玩味此语，我们不难看到，李白的回答也是有所寓意的。早在我国春秋战国时期的庄子，就在他的《外物篇》中描述过任公子钓巨鳌的故事。李白只不过是借历史典故，以任公子自喻，寄托自己的恢宏志向和抒发自己的远大抱负罢了。

垂钓能陶冶人的情操，抒发人的志向，锻炼人们的体魄，更能用它融情寓志，无怪乎当今钓风盛行。

千百年后，苏东坡评价李白："戏万乘若僚友，视俦列如草芥。"一番气壮山河、威慑群小的钓鱼高论把李白的侠肝义胆、闲情逸致表现得淋漓尽致。

23 The Fisherman Li Bai

It cannot be verified when fishing first began, but the transformation of fishing from a means of survival to a style of expressing emotions and cultivating one's tastes is really a great progress. The legend of Jiang Taigong fishing by the Weihe River 3,000 years ago is known to everybody. And Jiang Ziya held a fishing rod without a hook. Was he fishing purely for food or for pleasure? Surely, the latter.

So fishing became a style into which scholars of different times infused their feelings. Li Bai, a great poet who called himself a "fisherman", was one of them.

Although Li Bai was more than a famous poet, he was also an excellent fisherman. There are about 1,000 poetical works, among which more than 40 or 50 describe fishing or use fishing as a contrast. Some examples include "Afraid that the paddle disturb those gulls, leave the rod to wait for fishes" (from *Gushu Stream*) and "I can but poise a fishing pole beside a stream, or set sail for the sun like a sage in a dream" (from *One of the Three Poems Titled Hard is the Way of the World*).

Bold and unrestrained, Li Bai was extremely forthright and sincere to friends, but he never succumbed to those men of high ranks. Besides, he never forgot to sing the praises of the great rivers and mountains of his motherland. These personalities and thoughts are all reflected in his poems about fishing.

According to ancient writings, young Li Bai always enjoyed drinking, chanting poems, fishing and sword playing with friends of poems in Sichuan province, which he called the "Four types of fun of life". The great realist poet of the Tang Dynasty, Du Fu, praised Li Bai, "the verses will forever remain in the world, lived by gathering corals instead of fishing", which revealed that Li Bai had an affinity with fishing. Li Bai infused his feelings into fishing, which was not only a way that Li Bai used to express his feelings but also an outlet for feelings. Thus it made his verses remain forever in the world.

The great poet Li Bai once went fishing. There was a record in the sixth volume of *Records of Hou Qing* by Zhao Delin. Once, Li Bai went to the residence of the prime minster and presented one letter which read: "The fisherman Li Bai of the sea." The prime minster asked with a smile: "You fished near the sea, what are the hook and the fishing line made of?" Li Bai answered: "The moon is the hook, and the rainbow is fishing line." The prime minster asked again: "What is the bait?" Li Bai responded loudly: "It is made of the unrighteous officials." Li Bai's answer scared the prime minister.

Even in front of the famous prime minister, Li Bai called himself "fisherman", which revealed his high aspirations and fearlessness, and which also astonished the prime minister. Comparing himself to a fisherman, Li Bai expressed his great ambition of governing the county.

From what he said, "fishing by the bait which was made of unrighteous officials", we can feel the sense of "regarding the national affairs as his own duty". If Li Bai had had the right to control the country, he would have used those unrighteous officials as the bait for fishing, then the whole country would become cleaner and more peaceful.

Unfortunately, history did not unfold as he would have hoped. Pondering his words, we can easily figure out his implications. Early in the Spring and Autumn Period and the Warring States Period, Zhuangzi described the fishing story of Mr. Ren in his *Foreign Book*. Li Bai compared himself to Mr. Ren to express his great ambition.

By fishing, one can cultivate his tastes, express his ambitions and exercise his body. Besides, one can infuse his feelings into fishing, so no wonder it is still popular today.

Thousands of years later, Su Dongpo, the great poet in the Song Dynasty, praised Li Bai, "Treated the emperor as his colleague as well, but treated his colleagues like the real dirt", which vividly presents Li Bai's chivalrous and care-free personality and high aspirations from a grand viewpoint of fishing.

24 诗仙李白与诗圣杜甫相会的故事

韩愈云："李杜文章在，光焰万丈长。"李白是"诗仙"，杜甫是"诗圣"，仙、圣二字不只体现其作品、文学地位，更是其性格之写照。文士往来原本平常，尤其是在骑马仗剑走天涯的唐代。但因为当事人分别是诗仙、诗圣，这段交往的故事便被后人越来越关注。

天宝三年（744年）春夏之交，杜甫在洛阳遇到了大诗人李白。

那时，李白44岁，杜甫33岁。李白因为遭到谗毁，被唐玄宗"赐金""诏许还山"，实际上是被排挤出去，并且被要求离开长安。李白带着十分愤懑的心情从长安到了洛阳。

李白曾满怀信心和希望来到长安。到了长安后，李白确实受到了很高的礼遇。唐玄宗从金銮殿上下来，满面笑容，迎接李白，和李白亲切交谈，封李白为翰林学士。但唐玄宗只看重李白的诗文才华，翰林学士并非实际官职，没有实权，形同摆设，与李白的期望相距太远。李白的政治抱负不能得到施展，又不肯投靠朝中权贵，加上性格狂傲，容易得罪人，处境越来越困难，心情越来越压抑，只好整日纵酒狂歌。几年后，杜甫在诗中还写到当年李白豪放嗜酒的情景："李白斗酒诗百篇，长安市上酒家眠。天子呼来不上船，自称臣是酒中仙。"（《饮中八仙歌》）李白还写了一些诗抒发胸中的愤懑，其中《清平调》三首被一些小人别有用心地看作是讥讽杨贵妃，因而遭到了杨贵妃、高力士等人的谗毁。

高力士是唐玄宗最宠信的宦官。传说唐玄宗宴请李白时，李白酒醉，竟喝令高力士替他脱靴，高力士深以为耻，怀恨在心，便怂恿杨贵妃在唐玄宗面前诋毁李白。听信于杨贵妃的唐玄宗终于下诏，让李白离开长安。

杜甫在洛阳见到李白，写了一首《赠李白》的诗，诗中说，自己在东都洛阳已经进进出出两年了，看到的尽是投机取巧、尔虞我诈之事，感到十分厌恶。他想去学道求仙，但却没有碰到可以引荐的道士或仙人。现在好了，李白来到洛阳，自己可以和他一起去漫游梁宋（今河南开封一带），一起寻找那些道山仙境采摘瑶草了。

两位诗人见面后，决定一起去漫游。这年秋天，他们乘一叶轻舟，渡过波涛汹涌的黄河，到王屋山去拜访著名的道士华盖君，谁知华盖君已经去世，只遇见华盖君的几个弟子。两人看到观内一片狼藉，香灰满地，连炼丹的火也熄灭了，不禁伤心落泪。王屋山中野兽出没，咆哮不止，满眼荒凉，两人只得失望返回。

不久，李白与杜甫在梁宋漫游时，另一位著名诗人高适也加入了他们的行列。杜甫曾经在汶水见过高适，现在久别重逢，当然格外高兴。

高适是渤海（今河北景县一带）人，生于702年，此时已43岁。高适少年时家境贫寒，在梁宋一带流浪，甚至向人求乞。20岁时到了长安，本来想获取官职，却失望而归。后来，到过蓟门（今北京西南），想在边疆从军报国，立功沙场，虽然没有实现理想，却有了边疆生活的体验，创作了杰出的边塞诗《燕歌行》，因而在诗坛上名声大噪。

虽然李白和高适的才华极高，早已诗名远扬，但与年龄小得多的杜甫结交，仍然感到很高兴。杜甫和李白、高适会合在一起，同行同住，一同喝酒，谈论古今，品评人物，吟咏诗赋。三人都心高气傲，怀有豪情壮志，有着满腹才华，却都怀才不遇，功名不显，因而彼此间有着很多共同的话题。他们出入梁园（今河南开封）的酒店，痛饮畅谈，又趁着酒兴，一起登上城东南的吹台，望着辽阔的原野，想起汉高祖刘邦曾经在远处的芒山、砀山一带藏匿过，后来创立了伟大的事业，而现在古人何在，荒野上空有几只大雁和野鸭在呼叫。在傍晚寒风中，他们登上宋州（今河南商丘）以北的单父台（在今山东单县），遥望无边无际的原野，好像一直连到渤海边，万里风云扑面而来。寒风卷动着桑柘的落叶，野草随风在空中飞旋，尽管霜寒冰冻，他们仍然兴致勃勃，一起驰骋游猎，追逐飞禽走兽。

那时的宋州，名声虽然没有陈留（今河南开封）大，但仍是一个繁荣兴旺又充满着豪侠气息的城市。宋州人口稠密，楼台高大，街道宽广，舟车来自四面八方。当地人十分好客仗义，慷慨任侠，疾恶如仇，路见不平，拔刀相助。为了报仇，敢在闹市杀人；为了报恩，能毫不犹豫就倾其所有。

这种环境氛围，正符合激情四溢、热血沸腾、向往豪侠行为的三位诗人的心性。

天宝四年（745年）初，三位诗人离开了这里，高适到南方漫游，李白和杜甫北上齐州（今山东济南）。李白到了齐州紫极宫。杜甫拜见了北海（今山东益都）太守李邕。李邕因为不畏强权，敢于反对武则天宠信的张宗昌而冒犯武则天，在青年时期就有了很大的名气。李邕的文章、诗歌和书法在当时都享有盛名，特别擅长写墓志铭和碑文，虽然他长时间在外地任职，但朝廷中的很多士大夫、著名寺观的僧人道士，都携带钱物，专程到他的任所，请他写文章，他因此而获得大量馈赠。当时人们议论说，自古以来，以写文章获取大量财物的，没有一个比得上李邕。李邕仗义疏财，常常接济贫困的人，家中实际上没有多少财产。

他豪放奢侈，不拘小节，喜欢结交文士诗人。有一次，他得罪了当朝权相，被关在监狱，定了死罪，竟然有人上书唐玄宗愿意代替他死。李邕到了长安、洛阳，只要在街上走一走，就有很多人慕名跟随。李邕虽比杜甫大34岁，但很看重杜甫的才华，曾经主动结识杜甫，邀他一起谈论诗文。

这一年的秋天，杜甫到了兖州。李白也从任城（今山东济宁）来到兖州，与杜甫会合。杜甫写了一首绝句《赠李白》：

"秋来相顾尚飘蓬，未就丹砂愧葛洪。

痛饮狂歌空度日，飞扬跋扈为谁雄？"

当时，李白曾写过一首《戏赠杜甫》：

"饭颗山上逢杜甫，头戴笠子日卓午。

借问别来太瘦生？只为从前作诗苦。"

两个诗人秋天再一次见面时，都仍在漫游漂泊，就像在秋风中飘飞不定的蓬草。李白要想从失意和痛苦之中挣脱出来，追求得道成仙，实际上是做不到的。他无法像东晋的葛洪那样炼丹成仙，就只有整日痛饮狂歌，发泄心中的郁闷。李白如此狂放不羁，任性逞强，那是为什么呢？应该是因为英雄无用武之地，政治抱负无从实现的缘故吧！这首诗写的不仅是李白，实际上也是杜甫自己的处境和心情。

李白和杜甫一起上东蒙山，访问道士元逸人、董炼师。又一起到兖州城北寻访范隐士。范隐士的住处四周云烟缭绕，听得见寒杵声声，高大的树上结满了酸枣，寒瓜的藤蔓爬满了篱笆。两位诗人像亲兄弟一样，白天携手同行，一边喝酒，一边细细地谈论诗文，喝醉的时候便同被共眠。

杜甫与李白虽然整天地痛饮狂歌，访仙寻道，但力求在政治上大展宏图的愿望却一直没有熄灭。杜甫决定到长安去求取功名，李白也要到南方去，两人就在城东石门道别。

李白写了一首诗送给杜甫，记述了两人一起漫游的生活，希望有朝一日能重逢畅饮。分别后不久，李白在沙丘（今山东临清）又写了一首怀念杜甫的诗，说思念杜甫的感情就像浩荡的汶水一样，奔流不息。

两人分别后，再也没有机会见面，但杜甫一直很怀念李白，十分珍重这份友谊，无论在什么地方，他都常常想起李白来，写了不少怀念李白的诗。在两人传世的诗文中，李白写给杜甫的诗有3首，杜甫写给李白的诗有15首。

唐代文学史上两个最伟大的诗人，也是中国文学史上的伟大诗人——李白和杜甫结伴漫游和深厚友谊，成了中国文化史上的一段佳话。按闻一多的说法，"在我们四千年历史里，除了孔子见老子（假如他们是见过面的），没有比这两人的会面，更重大，更神圣，更可纪念的"。李白和杜甫两人的见面，就像"青天里太阳和月亮走碰了头"。

24 Immortal Poet Li Bai Meets Saint Poet Du Fu

"Like radiance, the poems of Li and Du spread far and wide." This was what Han Yu wrote to describe these two great poets. In fact, Li Bai was called the "Immortal Poet" and Du fu the "Saint Poet" because of their poems, literary status and personalities. In the Tang Dynasty, it was very common for people to travel everywhere on a horse with a sword, so the social communication between scholars also became commonplace. However, this meeting story between Li and Du—two of China's most famous poets—has become more and more attractive to later generations.

During the third year of Tianbao (744 A.D.), Du Fu met the great poet Li Bai in Luoyang at the turn of spring and summer.

That year, Li Bai was 44 years old and Du Fu 33. Due to the unhappy experiences of being slandered, Li Bai was not allowed to go back without permission of Emperor Xuanzong. In fact, he was expelled from the imperial court, and was even forced to leave Chang'an. In despair, Li Bai left Chang'an for Luoyang with frustration and resentment.

Originally, Li Bai came to Chang'an full of hope and confidence. At that time, Li Bai was really appreciated by Emperor Xuanzong, who could walk down the throne room with a big smile on his face to greet Li Bai and communicate with him. Although he was appointed as Hanlin Scholar, Li Bai had no real power. Everything seemed to go beyond his expectation. Emperor Xuanzong just valued nothing but his talent for poetry. So he had no chance to realise his political ambition, but he remained reluctant to follow those officials. On the other hand, his arrogant personality was not accepted by others. Finally, as the situation grew gloomy, he became so depressed that he indulged himself in drinking and singing, which was described by Du Fu several years later in *Eight Immortal Drinkers*: "Li Bai could turn sweet nectar into verses fine; drunk in the capital, he'd lie in shops of wine. Even imperial summons proudly he'd decline, saying immortals could not leave the drink divine." (from *Eight Immortal Drinkers*). Li Bai himself also wrote some poems to express his depression and resentment, of which the best-known is the three stanzas of *The Beautiful Lady Yang*. Because of this poem, he was said to ridicule Lady Yang in the imperial court and was thus backbitten by those people with ulterior motives like Lady Yang and Gao Lishi.

Gao Lishi was a eunuch who was very much favoured and trusted by Emperor Xuanzong. It was said that Li Bai got drunk at a banquet hosted by the emperor. At the banquet he ordered Gao Lishi to take off boots for him, which made Gao feel so disgraceful that he hated Li Bai very much and convinced Lady Yang to defame Li Bai in front of Emperor Xuanzong. Finally, Emperor Xuanzong followed Lady Yang's slander and drove Li Bai out of Chang'an.

Afterwards, Du Fu met Li Bai in Luoyang, and wrote *To Li Bai*. In this poem, he described that within the two years he stayed in the east capital, Luoyang, he witnessed cheating, lying and fraud, about which he felt extremely annoyed. He wanted to learn Taoism and pursue immortality. Unfortunately, it was hard for him to find a right guide. Just at this time, Li Bai arrived in Luoyang, so he could travel to Liangsong (in present Kaifeng city, Henan province) together with Li Bai and visited those mountains and learn Taoism.

The two poets decided to travel around the world together after they met. In the autumn of the third year of Tianbao, they crossed the mighty Yellow River by a small canoe to Mount Wangwu to pay a visit to the famous Taoist Hua Gaijun, who unfortunately had passed away. Seeing the monastery in a big mess and full of incense ash and Mount Wangwu surrounded by roaring wild animals, they both could not help sheding tears from sadness.

Not long after, another famous poet Gao Shi joined them in Liangsong. Du Fu had met Gao Shi in Wenshui before, so he was especially glad to meet him again after a long time of separation.

Gao Shi, 43 years old then, was born in 707 in Bohai (in present Jing county, Hebei province). Born into a poor family, young Gao Shi led a wandering life in Liangsong and even had to beg for a living. He went to Chang'an at 20 for an official position, but returned with dissappointment. Later, he went to Jinmen (in present southwest Beijing), intending to realise his political dream of joining the army to make contributions to his country. Although he couldn't realise his ambition, he accumulated some experiences of frontier life, which brought him his masterpiece *A Song of the Yan Country*, for which he rose to fame in the poetic world.

Although Li Bai and Gao Shi were well-known for their poetry, they were still glad to make friends with younger Du Fu. They three met together whilst traveling and they soon began living together, drinking, talking about everything ancient and modern, commenting on famous figures and chanting poems. They had a lot in common because of their proud and arrogant personalities, lofty sentiments and aspirations and great talents, which couldn't be recognized by others. They often went to Liangyuan pub (in present Kaifeng, Henan province) to drink and talk to their hearts' content. They also climbed to the performance platform located in the southeast of the city when getting drunk. Looking at the vast fields, they recalled Liu Bang, who once hid in the area of Mount Mang and Mount Dang but he still founded a great country. But where were those ancients? Nowhere were they found except for several wild geese and ducks. On a cold evening, when they climbed the Shanfu platform (in present Shan county, Shandong province) located in Songzhou (present Shangqiu, Henan province), what they saw in the distance were the vast fields extending to the Bohai Sea, and what they encountered was the chilly wind blowing on their faces. Although the leaves of Sangzhe and the wild grasses were fluttering in the frostbite frozen cold air, they were still in high spirits and enjoyed running and chasing wild animals and birds.

Songzhou used to be a prosperous city full of human kindness. Although it was not as famous as Chenliu (present Kaifeng, Henan province), it was a densely populated city with tall buildings and wide streets. People there were extremely hospitable, generous and helpful. They were ready to help those in need or those who were unfairly treated. They would also kill their enemies in public for revenge or would pour all they had to repay an obligation.

That kind of environment and atmosphere was especially agreeable to the temperament of these three energetic and passionate poets who were eager for heroic acts.

At the beginning of the fourth year of Tianbao (745 A.D.), these three poets left Songzhou. Gao Shi traveled to the south, but Li Bai and Du Fu headed north for Qizhou (in present Jinan, Shandong province). Li Bai arrived in Ziji Palace of Qizhou, and Du Fu went to visit Li Yong who is the Prefecture of Beihai (in present Yidu, Shandong province). Li Yong was well-known for defying political power in his youth, and he offended Empress Wu Zetian and her courtier Zhang Zongchang. Li Yong also had a good reputation for his articles, poems and handwriting, and he was especially good at writing epitaphs and inscriptions. Although he served at other places, a lot of officials from the imperial court and monks and Taoists of famous temples paid a special visit to his home and invited him to write articles, so he got considerable rewards. It was said at that time that no one could gain so much by writing articles than Li Yong. But Li Yong really had no significant wealth because he was generous in aiding needy people, especially those poor people.

Due to his passionate and unconstrained personality, he liked to make friends with scholars and poets. Once, he was put in prison as a punishment for offending the prime minister of the Tang Dynasty. Strangely enough, there was someone who submitted a statement to Emperor Xuanzong expressing his willingness to replace Li Yong to die. When he wandered the streets of Chang'an and Luoyang, he would surely be followed by a lot of fans. Although he was 34 years older than Du Fu, he appreciated Du Fu's talent and wanted to make friends and to talk about poems with him.

In the autumn of that same year, Du Fu arrived in Yanzhou. Li Bai also came to Yanzhou from Rencheng (in present Jining, Shandong province) to meet Du Fu. For this, Du Fu wrote *To Li Bai*:

"When autumn comes, you're drifting still like thistledown;
You try to find the way to Heaven, but you fail.
In singing mad and drinking dead your days you drown.
O when will fly the roc, and when will leap the whale?"

And Li Bai also wrote a poem titled *Addressed Humorously to Du Fu*:

"On top of Hill of Boiled Rice I met Du Fu,
Who in the noonday sun wore a hat of bamboo.
Pray, how could you have grown so thin since we did part?
Is it because the verse composing wrung your heart?"

When the two poets met again in autumn, they were still wandering lonely like drifting clouds. Therefore, it was actually impossible for Li Bai to escape from frustrations and pains by pursuing spiritual freedom in Taoism. He couldn't become an immortal like Ge Hong, who was a great master of the Eastern Jin Dynasty. So he drank and sang with wild joy to relieve his depression. Why did Li Bai become an arrogant, unrestrained and self-willed person? The reason must be that there were no opportunities for him to put his talents to good use and to realise his political ambition. This poem not only was a self-portrait of Li Bai but also a depiction of the situation and mood of Du Fu himself.

Li Bai and Du Fu went to Mount Dongmeng to visit Taoists Yuan Yiren and

Dong Lianshi and then visited hermit Fan who lived in the north of Yanzhou city. The residence of hermit Fan was surrounded by cloud and mist. Everywhere was filled with tranquilness except for the chilly sound of wooden knocker in the temple. The huge trees were covered with sour jujubes and the fence was enlaced by melon cirrus. The two poets always gathered there walking, drinking, talking about poetry like brothers, even sleeping together when getting drunk.

Although Li Bai and Du Fu drank wine and chanted poems and visited immortals and Taoists every day, they didn't give up their political ambition. Finally, Du Fu decided to go to Chang'an to seek an official position, and Li Bai also planned to go to the south. So they made a farewell at the Stone Gate of the east of the city.

Li Bai wrote one poem to Du Fu, which mainly described their wandering life together and his wishes to meet again. Shortly after they got separated, Li Bai wrote another poem expressing how he missed Du Fu in Shaqiu (in present Linqing, Shandong province), which was like the ever-flowing Wenshui River.

Although they hadn't seen each other since that time, Du Fu always missed Li Bai and thought of him wherever he was. He treasured the friendship between them so much that he also created many poems expressing his longing for Li Bai. Among all their poems handed down, 3 were written by Li Bai for Du Fu while 15 by Du Fu for Li Bai.

The wandering experiences together and profound friendship between Li Bai and Du Fu—the two most famous poets of the Tang Dynasty literature history and of the Chinese literature history—became an interesting story on everybody's lips. According to Wen Yiduo, "no other meeting in our 4,000 years of history was more important, holy and memorable than that between Li Bai and Du Fu except that between Confucius and Laozi (if they did meet)". As was joked, their meeting was momentous, like the sun meeting the moon in the sky.

25 李白与"太白酒"的故事

相传唐朝时，重庆万州名叫南浦。安史之乱时，李白因辅佐永王李璘，得罪朝廷，流放夜郎。途中经过南浦，因长途跋涉，艰辛劳累，李白病倒了，就在南浦的西岩休养了一段时间。

李白当时心情十分忧郁，想到自己雄才大志未得实现，反遭奸臣陷害，他多么想痛饮几杯，醉卧三天，忘却一切忧虑，在诗和酒中寻找安慰啊。怎奈这南浦乃偏僻之地，既没有知心朋友唱和，也没有可口的好酒消愁。

当时南浦有个县令，名叫秦禄，此人不务正业，下棋成癖。他闻知李白不仅诗才盖世，而且精通棋艺，便时常来找李白下棋。李白为了消磨时日，也乐得与他对弈消遣。

秦县令自恃棋艺是南浦之冠，不把李白放在眼里。一天，他请来南浦全城的棋手，当众和李白对棋，想打败李白，更进一步显示他的棋艺。结果出乎意外，李白得胜，县令惨败。县令气得酱色的脸一下变青，幸亏有善于给主子拍马屁的师爷给他圆场，说："这回不算数，下次再来。"县令虽强作镇静，但也难免怒形于色。

县令当众丢了面子，五脏六腑都气炸了。他忙把师爷叫来商量对策，说："我是一个堂堂县令，李白乃是一个被贬谪的罪人，我竟被他打败，今后我这父母官还有什么威风？"

师爷献媚地说："老爷休气，胜败乃兵家常事。不过依下官看来，李白来自京都，见过全国各家名手，棋艺确实非凡，老爷想胜过他也有难处。今下官有一条妙计，下次去西门外酒坊里，买回两坛劲儿大的酒，先请李白喝酒，把他灌醉，再找他对棋，他昏昏沉沉，棋数必乱，老爷要战败他就容易了。"县令一听，喜上眉梢，连声喊："好！好！好！"

县令得到师爷的妙计，立即把听差叫到面前，吩咐道："明天你去西门外酒坊挑两坛酒来，下次我和李白对棋时，先请他喝酒，你在一旁斟酒，看我的眼色行事，尽量给李白多斟，灌他个烂醉如泥。"听差连连点头，声称"照办！照办！"

听差原是个穷苦人，他心地善良，从不忍心欺负百姓，敲诈良民。他也去看过李白下棋，佩服李白的棋艺高超。他听了县令说的这套诡计，心中甚是不平。不忍心看到这个被奸臣陷害的可怜文人，再受县令的欺凌。因此，他表面答应县令的吩咐，暗中却琢磨着如何保护这个远方来的客人。

听差来到酒坊，替县令买酒，酒坊老板岂敢怠慢，按照吩咐挑选了两坛。此酒劲头特大，不会喝酒的人，一杯即醉；善于饮酒的人，三五杯也便醉倒。听差想：李白身体本有病，要是喝上三杯五盏，不但下棋不灵，而且还会加重病症，甚至性命难保。他挑着酒坛不知不觉来到天仙桥，见从歇凤山岩缝里流淌出来的泉水清澈纯净，晶莹透亮，汇成一股小溪，流过这天仙桥。他想，何不冲点泉水在酒里，把浓酒冲淡，让李太白喝了不醉，也许可以幸免灾难。于是，趁无人之机，揭开酒坛，捧了许多泉水倒进酒坛里，又从从容容地挑回县衙去了。

这天，县令请来更多的棋手，声称正式和李白决一胜负，并扬言如果输了，就不当县令。

下棋之前，县令假惺惺地对李白说："本官闻知先生好饮酒，特备上本地特产上等头酒，请先生好好品尝品尝。美酒助兴，定会显出更精湛的棋艺来。"说罢，举杯和李白对饮。听差按照县官的吩咐，在一旁斟酒。李白饮了一杯又一杯，而县令却只是做做样子，饮得很少。

喝了酒以后，李白兴致勃勃，精神百倍，不但没有昏昏沉沉，而且神志更加清醒，棋法更精，稳重灵活，攻势猛烈。秦县令只有招架之功，哪有还手之力。斗了几个回合，秦县令落得惨败。

秦县令垂头丧气回到县衙，满腹怨怒，有气无处泄。过了一会儿他静下心来，感到事情不免有些蹊跷，这样的头酒，身强力壮的小伙子喝几杯也要醉倒，体弱多病的李白竟然如喝白开水一般，毫无醉意。想到刚才自己喝的时候，也不觉有醉意，似乎这酒变淡了，原来那股辣味也没有了，而且绵软清香。县官琢磨着，又去舀一杯来品尝，果然香气扑鼻，绵软可口，和过去买的酒大不一样。香甜的美酒，立刻冲淡了县令满肚子怒气，他忙把听差唤来，瞪着眼睛问道："你前日是从何处买来的酒，如实说来！"

听差听了，身躯微微颤抖，唯恐兑水之事被老爷发觉，连忙答应道："秦老爷，奴才是从西门外酒坊买来的酒，一点不差。"

"你别骗我，西门酒坊的酒我尝得出来，哪有这般美味？究竟是从何处买的，如实招来。"

听差颇觉奇怪，左思右想也不知酒怎么会变好的，他忽然醒悟道：是不是因为兑了天仙桥下的溪水呢？他只好把兑水一事招了出来，县令一听忙叫人一起再去试试。一试果然如此。

这件事流传开了，于是酒坊都采用天仙桥的溪水酿酒，酿出了很多美酒来。

李白得此美酒，一日三饮，心爽神怡，精神倍增，郁闷顿消，疾病痊愈，住在南浦，不愿离去。传说，李白后来没去夜郎，因喝了南浦美酒成了仙人。

从此，南浦名酒一代代传了下来。为了纪念李白，人们就把"南浦酒"改名为"太白酒"。

25 Li Bai and "Taibai Wine"

It is said that in the Tang Dynasty, present Wanzhou in Chongqing Municipality was called Nanpu. During the Anshi Rebellion, Li Bai offended the emperor, because he joined the loyal force led by Prince Yong—Li Lin, so he was banished to Yelang. After a long and hard march, Li Bai fell ill. Then, he had to rest himself at Xiyan of Nanpu for a while.

At that moment, depressed and hopeless, Li Bai wanted to drown his sorrows through drinking and sleeping when he thought of his experiences and unrealized ambition. But Nanpu was an isolated county where there were neither good friends nor good wine.

Qin Lu was the county magistrate of Nanpu, and he seemed to have nothing to do except play chess. He often played chess with Li Bai when he learned about his poetic talents and chess skills. Playing chess with Qin Lu was an acceptable way to kill time, so Li Bai did not refuse to play with him.

Qin Lu was so confident in his best chess skills in Nanpu that he showed contempt in Li Bai. One day, he gathered all the chess players and wanted to demonstrate his excellent chess skills in front of them by defeating Li Bai. Unexpectedly, Li Bai was the winner. So the county magistrate was outraged because of his repeated failures, but fortunately one private adviser was good at flattery, "This round does not count, let's take the next round," he added. Finally, the county magistrate forced himself to calm down , but failed to cover his anger.

Losing face in public, the county magistrate was really furious. So he summoned the private adviser to discuss: "As the county magistrate, I was defeated by Li Bai who was a guilty man. How could I keep my dignity in front of my people?"

In order to please the county magistrate, the private adviser said: "Don't get angry. It's common for you to win or to lose. In my humble opinion, Li Bai came from Chang'an where famous players from different places gather, so his chess skills are really extraordinary. I have an idea that we just need to buy two jars of strong wine in the winery outside the west gate. You can invite him to drink wine, and play chess with him when he gets drunk. Then you will defeat him easily." The county magistrate was satisfied with this advice, so he shouted loudly: "Good idea!"

The county magistrate called the gofer and said: "You buy two jars of wine in the winery outside the west gate tomorrow. And you need to pour out wine for Li Bai when I play chess with him next time. You should act upon my hint and try your best to make him drunk." The servant nodded and answered: "All right! All right!"

In fact, the gofer was poor but kind. And he never did any harm like hurting and blackmailing ordinary people. He admired Li Bai for his chess skills. So he was annoyed with the tricks of the county magistrate and couldn't bear to see the poor scholar teased by the treacherous county magistrate. Consequently, he accepted the order of the county magistrate but wondered how to secretly protect the guest.

The gofer came to the winery to buy wine for the county magistrate, so the boss quickly selected two jars of wine. This wine was strong enough to get an ordinary person drunk with one cup and a tippler drunk with three to five cups. The gofer thought Li Bai would lose the capability of playing chess well or even lose life if he drank three to five cups. He unconsciously came to the Tianxian Bridge with the two jars of wine. He saw clean spring water flowing from Mount Xiefeng to a stream and crossing the bridge with long nice sound. Then a good idea occurred to him: why don't I mix some water in the wine? If the wine was not so strong, Li Bai might survive. So he opened the jars and poured some water into the them secretly, then took the wine to the county *yamen* unhurriedly.

The day came when the county magistrate invited more chess players, and claimed he would make a final bid for victory over Li Bai and if he lost, he would resign.

Before the contest, the county magistrate hypocritically said to Li Bai: "I know you like drinking, so I have prepared the local wine for you. Good wine helps to play chess well." Then, they began to drink with the gofer serving Li Bai with one cup after another in accordance with the instructions of the county magistrate. So Li Bai drank a lot but the county magistrate drank just a little.

After drinking some wine, Li Bai felt more energetic and conscious, which the county magistrate had not expected. Li Bai's chess skills became more exquisite and flexible. In this case, the county magistrate could only protect himself and got no chance to fight back. After several rounds, Li Bai completely defeated the county magistrate.

The county magistrate went back to his office full of anger, having nowhere to release his resentment. Then he calmed down and thought what had happened was strange. In fact, even a strong man may not hold it, but sick Li Bai could drink it like water without getting drunk. And he remembered that he was clearly not intoxicated when he drank the wine. The aroma of it seemed to fade, and the fiery taste disappeared. So the county magistrate filled another glass and tasted it. Sure enough, it tasted good and was different from the wine he had drunk before. The good wine also defused his anger. He called the gofer and asked with glaring eyes: "Where did you buy the wine? Tell me the truth!"

The gofer could not help trembling, for fear of being discovered by the county magistrate. So he responded hurriedly: "My lord, I bought it from the winery outside the west gate. No problem at all."

"You are lying! I know the wine flavour in that winery, it cannot compare with this wine. Tell me the truth, where did you buy it?" the county magistrate shouted.

The gofer also felt very strange: "How could the wine become so tasty?" He suddenly realised that it was possibly due to the water under the Tianxian Bridge. So he confessed what he had done. The county magistrate asked others to try it again and then found the secret.

This story was spread so widely that many wineries began to use the water under the Tianxian Bridge to make good wine.

After getting the wine, Li Bai drank three times a day. And soon he became more energetic and refreshed, and recovered from his illness. So he was unwilling to leave Nanpu. One legend holds that Li Bai didn't go to Yelang, because he became an immortal after drinking the good wine of Nanpu.

From then on, the famous wine of Nanpu passed down from one generation to another. And people renamed "Nanpu Wine" to "Tai Bai Wine" in memory of Li Bai.

26 "太白酒家"的故事

这一年，冬天刚到，就已寒气袭人。李白住在采石矶，他经常到街头的一家酒店里去沽酒。这酒店是一个姓鲁的财主开的，人们都叫他鲁老板。别看这鲁老板表面对人和颜悦色，骨子里却很心狠。他手捻佛珠，口诵阿弥陀佛，肚子里却时时打着小算盘，想着怎样盘剥他人。他家用的几个酒保，个个累得弯腰驼背，到头来，却都被他踢出门去。

这一天，李白又到酒店来沽酒。躺在椅子上的鲁老板捻着胡子，眯着眼，笑吟吟地打量着李白，心想：这个穷书生离开京都几年了，带来的钱大概花得差不多了。当初，李白头次进店，他笑脸相迎，以后常来常往，他估计榨不出多少油水了，脸色就一次比一次难看。

他暗示小酒保别理李白，可酒保偏偏热情地为李白斟酒，临走，还把上等美酒给李白灌上一大壶。这回，说什么也不能便宜李白了。他站起身，踱到李白身后，弦外有音地说："小店屋檐太低，酒池太浅，经不住翰林这样的大酒壶啊！"

李白明知上回给的酒钱还够沽几次，现在看鲁老板的这副模样，也不愿多同他争辩，就从怀里取出最后一锭银子往柜台上一掷，"啪"地震得鲁老板两眼发亮，满面乌云立时消散，浮出一片笑容，说："老朽有眼不识江底浅，没想到李翰林还有这么多酒钱。"他转身忙吩咐酒保说："快，快给大人沽酒，找大人银子！"

李白一挥袖子道："算了，下次再来！"鲁老板两眼眯成一道缝，一个劲地连说："是，是！"

第二天黄昏，李白又来了，酒保又为他满满灌上壶酒。第三天，第四天，李白天天一趟，鲁老爷很是不耐烦了，他算算李白丢下的一锭银子，再有个把月也差不多了，就用花言巧语支开酒保，偷偷地往李白酒壶里兑水。

李白喝了几口，觉得味道不够，但也没说什么。以后每次李白来，鲁老板总装得特别热情，亲自为李白灌酒，暗地里却多加了一倍水。一天天过去了，李白若无其事。后来鲁老板干脆给李白灌上满满一壶江水。

　　李白还以为是酒呢，路过独木桥时，几个顽童在河边扔石子，一块石子向李白飞来，他吓了一跳，忙把酒壶往怀里一搂："哎哟，别把我的酒壶打翻了！"逗得几个顽童哈哈大笑。来到船上，李白拎起酒壶往杯子里倒，一闻，味道不对；喝一口，"呸"地吐了出来！一看，才知是又浊又浑的江水。

　　他气坏了，想找鲁老板去理论，又一想，和这种人没什么好讲的。唉，无奈采石矶这一带就这一家酒店。求他施舍，不行！就是在皇帝老爷面前，李白也不曾低三下四过，更何况对这样一个小人！

　　更深夜静，他翻来覆去地睡不稳，想写点诗，又写不出。多年来，酒和他结下不解之缘。一壶酒下肚，他便能暂时忘记愁苦，把雾蒙蒙的世界，看个清清楚楚。可是如今，在这满目凄凉的采石矶头，连唯一能使他解闷的酒都没有了！

　　"李白斗酒诗百篇"，没有酒，就写不出诗来。他叹了口气，静听着房檐下淅淅沥沥的雨滴声，心都要碎了。

　　第二天，李白路过一间茅舍，一位两鬓全白的老人，朝他点头微笑，热情地邀请他到屋里去坐。刚一进门，老人就朝李白拜了下去："感谢救命恩人！"

　　李白呆立着，不知是怎么回事。老汉含着泪诉说道："我姓纪，老家在幽州。那年遭灾荒，我和老伴带着孩子上山剥树皮。忽然出现了两只吊睛白额大虎扑上来，把我那老伴吃了，我和孩子吓得魂不附体。多亏先生您正好在那里游玩，飞起一箭，连射两虎，我父子俩才得以死里逃生。"

　　李白听了恍然大悟，连忙扶起老汉说："算不得什么，算不得什么。"

　　老汉说："多年来，为了报恩，我暗地跟着您，除了您在京都时，我进不了皇宫外，从金陵到庐州，从宣城到采石矶，我一直跟在您身边，捕鱼，打柴。"

　　李白听了，热泪盈眶，一把拉住老人的手，亲切地问："孩子呢？"

　　老人顺手一指说："在酒店里帮工。"

李白正想把鲁老板以水当酒的事告诉老人，老人打断他说："我已听孩子讲啦。这种只看得到钱的人，是什么事都做得出来。"说罢，从屋里抱出一大坛子酒对李白说："来，恩人，开怀畅饮吧！"老人拍拍胸说："往后，您喝的酒，全由我这老头子包啦！"

李白乐得不知如何是好，憋了多天的酒瘾，一下子全冲了出来。他等不得老人拿菜出来，就端起杯来一饮而尽。饮着，饮着，就醉了。他眯着醉眼，跌跌撞撞地跑到门外的"联璧台"上，叫人拿笔，老人知道李白诗兴大发，就赶快递上准备好的笔墨纸张。遥望着滚滚的大江，如血的落日，李白提起笔来，一挥而就：

"天门中断楚江开，碧水东流至此回。

两岸青山相对出，孤帆一片日边来。"

老人伸出颤抖的双手，捧起墨迹未干的草书，奔回茅屋，恭恭敬敬地贴在了墙上。

打那起，这间普通的茅屋可热闹起来了。过路的、打柴的、捕鱼的，都想进来看看墙上的诗。有的抄，有的背，一传十，十传百。有的还千里迢迢，专门来欣赏这首诗。有人问起是谁写的，老汉总竖起拇指，自豪地对大家说："是仙人李白的手迹。他是喝了我酿的酒，才写出这般好诗的呀！"

一听这话，南来北往的人都争着到这里，坐下喝两盅，细细品味着这醉人的美酒，领略着诗人创造的意境……也不知从哪天起老汉开起了酒店，不分日夜，除了为李白酿酒，还用甘甜的美酒为客人洗去一路的风尘。

从此，"太白酒家"的店号就亮了出来。

俗话说，"同行是冤家"。那个鲁老板听说姓纪的白发老头酿酒手艺高超，生意兴隆，一肚子的不快。加上小酒保宁愿不要半年工钱也要跑到太白酒家去帮工，闹得自家酒店门庭冷落，气得他吹胡子瞪眼。他左思右想也没法子，只得叫家人捧着几只大元宝，再带上两坛美酒，亲自到江边去拜访李白，想请他写一首诗，为自己撑撑门面。

李白一眼看出这位鲁老板的来意，冲他摆摆手："你家酒池太浅，经不住我一口喝的啊！"说罢把手一扬，叫船翁开船篙一点，小船轻轻离开江岸，朝江心驶去。随着李白的歌声，那高大的身影渐渐融进了落日的余晖里。

鲁老板急得像热锅上的蚂蚁，嘶哑着喉咙喊道："仙人哪仙人，你停停，有话好说，好说呀！"跑了几步，被石头绊了一下"扑通"一声倒在了沙滩上。

不久，鲁家酒店关门了，而纪老汉的"太白酒家"生意一天旺似一天。一年后，纪老汉不幸病故，李白悲痛欲绝，把酒洒进长江，整整哭了三天三夜，并且写下一首悼念纪老汉的诗《哭宣城善酿纪叟》：

"纪叟黄泉里，还应酿老春。

夜台无李白，沽酒与何人？"

可见，李白与酿酒老汉情谊多么深厚啊！

千百年来，沿江一带，许多大大小小的酒店总以"太白酒家""太白遗风"作为店号，用布写好挑在门前檐下，以表达对伟大诗人李白的纪念之情。

26 The Story about "Tai Bai Wineshop"

When winter came, it was already very cold. Li Bai lived in Caishiji, and he often bought wine from one wineshop run by a man whose family name was Lu, so he was called Boss Lu. Although the boss superficially showed kindness to people, he was a totally ruthless man. He seemed to like practicing Buddhism on the surface, but inwardly thought about his own profits. So how to exploit others became his main job. For example, Boss Lu's diligent attendants were finally fired by him when they were unable to work for him any more.

One day, Li Bai went to the wineshop to buy wine again. Lying on the chair, Boss Lu twirled his moustache and looked at Li Bai with a smile, thinking that the poor scholar might now run out of his money since he has been away from the capital for several years. He greeted Li Bai with a broad smile at the first time, then with time going and Li Bai's money being spent off, he knew he could not make any more profits from Li Bai, so he became more and more indifferent to him.

Boss Lu hinted that the attendant should not entertain Li Bai, but the attendant still enthusiastically poured wine for him. He even filled Li Bai's wine pot when he left. Seeing this, the Boss thought he would take this chance to get profits from Li Bai. So he stood up and walked to Li Bai, saying with irony: "My shop was too small to satisfy you!"

Li Bai knew that the money he paid last time was still enough to cover his costs this time. Looking at the Boss, he decided not to argue with him, so he took out one ingot silver from his bosom and threw it on the counter with a bang. Hearing the sound, Boss Lu's eyes lit up and said with a smile: "Blame me, for I fail to know people very well, I really didn't know you had so much money." Then he turned to the attendant and said: "Hurry up, pour wine for our guest and give him the change!"

Li Bai swung his sleeves and said: "No, just keep it for next time!" Boss Lu smiled and kept responding: "Ok! Ok!"

The next evening, Li Bai went there again and the attendant filled his wine pot. Then Li Bai went there again the next day, and the next. Boss Lu became impatient because he thought the money left by Li Bai would run out in probably a month. So he asked the attendant to leave and added water to the wine for Li Bai.

After a few drinks, Li Bai found it tasted peculiar but said nothing. Since then, Boss Lu treated him with hospitality and poured wine in person, but doubled water in it secretly. Time passed by, and Li Bai acted as if nothing had happened. Afterwards, Boss Lu simply filled Li Bai's wine pot full with water.

However, Li Bai didn't detect the fraud and thought it was wine. When he passed the single-plank bridge, several naughty kids were throwing stones by the river side. Suddenly, one stone flew to Li Bai, he hurried to hold his wine pot in his arms: "Ah, don't knock over my wine pot!" making those naughty kids roar with laughter. When he came to a boat and poured the wine into a cup, a peculiar smell emitted from it. Sure enough, the taste was not right, so he spit it out, finding that it was muddy water.

133

Li Bai was so angry and intended to argue with Boss Lu, but he thought that there was nothing to say with such kind of person. Unfortunately, there was no other wineshop in this area. But begging Boss Lu for wine would not work. He had never done such a humble thing even in front of the emperor, so it was impossible for him to do so to such a vile person.

That night, he turned over in bed. Although he wanted to write poems, he had no inspiration without wine. After drinking, he could temporarily drown his sorrow and see the reality of the ugly world. However, living in this isolated Caishiji, he even could not get a drop of wine.

"Li Bai could turn sweet nectar into verses fine" meant that Li Bai could not write poems without wine. Listening to the rain dripping from the house roof, he sighed and felt heart-broken.

The next day, Li Bai met a grey-haired old man when passing by a cottage. The old man nodded and smiled and invited Li Bai to his home. The moment he walked in, the old man bowed down to Li Bai and said: "Thank you for saving my life!"

Li Bai stood still and did not know what had happened. The old man said with tears: "My family name is Ji, and my hometown is Youzhou. That year, we suffered natural disasters, my wife and I took our child to strip bark (as food) off trees in the mountain. Suddenly, two big tigers ran to us, and ate my wife. My child and I were scared out of wits. Fortunately, you shot them dead while you happened to stroll about there, so we both had a narrow escape from death."

Li Bai immediately understood and helped him to rise saying: "It is not worth mentioning."

The old man said: "In order to repay you, I always followed you secretly over the years. Of course, except the imperial palace in the capital, I followed you from Jinling to Luzhou, from Xuancheng to Caishiji, making a living by fishing and cutting trees."

Hearing this, Li Bai's eyes were filled with tears and asked him affectionately: "Where is the child?"

The old man pointed to the wineshop: "He is working there."

Li Bai was about to tell him about Boss Lu using water instead of wine when the old man interrupted: "I've learned about it from my child. Those who only care about money could do anything to benefit themselves." Then, he took out a big jar of wine and said to Li Bai: "From now on, I will provide all the wine for you!"

Li Bai was too excited to know what to do. He couldn't even hold the crutch of alcohol. So he began drinking before the dish was served. After a few drinks, he got drunk. Then he squinted and ran to the Lianbi Platform which was a great stone in Caishiji. The old man knew Li Bai got poetic when he asked for brush pen, so he quickly got the pen, ink and paper ready. Looking at the rolling river in distance and the red sunset, he wrote a poem at one go:

"Breaking Mount Heaven's Gate, the great river rolls through,
Its east-flowing green billows, hurled back here, turn north.
From the two river banks thrust out the mountains blue,
Leaving the sun behind, a lonely sail comes forth."

Holding the poet with trembling hands, the old man ran to his cottage before the ink was dry and posted it on the wall respectfully.

From then on, the ordinary hut became noisy. Everyone who passed it would come to appreciate the poem, including passersby, firewood people and fishermen. Some copied it, others recited it. News traveled fast and many people came here to appreciate the poem from far away. If someone asked who wrote it, the old man would gave him a thumb and said proudly: "It was the handwriting of the immortal poet Li Bai. He wrote such a good poem because he drank my wine!"

Hearing this, many people from different places poured here. They all wanted to taste the wine and appreciated the artistic conception. Nobody knows when the old man started his wine shop. He worked day and night making wine for Li

Bai and providing wine for all the guests.

Since then, the brand of "Tai Bai Wineshop" became famous.

As the saying goes, "two of a trade can never agree". Boss Lu was very angry when he heard the grey-haired old man was good at making excellent wine and also did brisk business. In addition, the attendant of his shop would rather work in Tai Bai Wineshop at the cost of giving up six months of wages. After a bit of brainstorming, he asked his family members to take several large gold ingots and two jars of good wine to visit Li Bai, begging him to write a poem to attract customers.

Li Bai recognized Boss Lu's purpose easily, so he declined the offer: "Your wine is not enough for me to drink!" Then, Li Bai waved and motioned to the boatman to sail. The small boat gently left the river bank and headed for the middle. With his singing, Li Bai's tall figure blended into the last glimmer of sunset.

Boss Lu shouted with a hoarse voice: "Immortal, please wait a moment. We can settle it in peace." After a few steps, he stumbled over a stone and fell on the river beach.

Soon the wineshop of Boss Lu was bankrupt, but Tai Bai Wineshop of Ji became more prosperous. A year later, Ji died of illness, Li Bai mourned and cried for three days and three nights. He poured wine into the Changjiang River, and wrote a poem titled *Elegy on Master Brewer Ji of Xuancheng* to mourn him:

"For thirsty souls are you still brewing,
Good wine of Old Spring, Master it?
In underworld are you not ruing,
To lose a connoisseur like me?"

From this poem, we can see the profound friendship between Li Bai and Brewer Ji.

For thousands of years, many big and small wineshops were always named as "Tai Bai Wineshop" and "Tai Bai Style". They put the shop name on a piece of cloth and hang it under the eaves in memory of the great poet Li Bai.

27 李白投宿五松山下的故事

到了晚年，李白的生活更加穷困潦倒，不得不靠朋友帮助度日。这样，他同劳动人民有了较多的接触，对他们产生了深厚的感情，写下了一些反映劳动人民生活的诗篇。

有一天傍晚，李白赶路来到五松山（在今安徽省）下，又累又饿，再也走不动了。他想找个地方住下来，问了几个大户人家，都不肯收留。

李白无可奈何地往前走去，在一座茅屋前面，他看见一位头发花白的老妇人正在洗野菜，就问道："大嫂，能在您家借住一夜吗？"

老妇人见李白是个穷苦的读书人，又看天已经快黑了，就点了点头。茅屋不大，只有两个房间。老妇人腾出一间，铺好床，又给李白打来洗脸水，就忙着做饭去了。

过了一会儿，老妇人端来一盘饭，说："先生，山里人家本来就苦，今年大旱，又颗粒无收，东家还来催租。实在没什么好东西招待，就请尝尝这慈姑（一种水生植物，果实可以吃）米饭，压压饥吧！"

李白刚才看见老妇人在洗野菜，知道这就是她家最好的吃食了。他心里非常感动，接过盘子，再三道谢。

夜深了，李白躺在床上，久久不能入睡。他看到农家劳苦的生活，受到他们热情真诚的接待，回想起官场的钩心斗角，人情淡薄，不由得感慨万分。

后来，李白写了《宿五松山下荀媪家》这首诗。他在诗中记述了这次借宿的情况，并且倾注了对这位老妇人的一片感激之情。

"我宿五松下，寂寥无所欢。

田家秋作苦，邻女夜舂寒。

137

跪进雕胡饭，月光明素盘。

令人惭漂母，三谢不能餐。"

27 Li Bai Spends One Night at the Foot of Mount Five Pines

In his later years, Li Bai lived a much poorer life and had to depend on friends for help. Therefore, he had more contact with working people and developed a deep affection for them, which was reflected in some of his poems.

One evening, Li Bai came to Mount Five Pines (in present Anhui province), tired and hungry, he could not move any further. He wanted to find a place to lodge in, but was refused by a few wealthy families.

Li Bai walked on hopelessly until he arrived at a hut. He saw a grey-haired old woman washing vegetables and asked: "Madame, can I spend the night in your home?"

Judging that Li Bai was a poor scholar and seeing the day getting dark, she nodded to accept his request. There were two rooms in the small hut. The old woman made a room for him. After making the bed and preparing a bath, the old woman went to cook for him.

After a while, the old woman brought him dinner and said: "Sir, as mountainous farmers, we really live a poor life. Especially in this drought year, the crops were ruined. Besides, the landlord also presses for the rent. So I don't have any delicious food to treat you, please have the wild rice to deal with your hunger!"

Seeing the old woman washing wild vegetables, Li Bai guessed that it must be the best food for her family. So he was very moved and thanked her repeatedly when he received the plate.

Late at night, Li Bai turned over in bed with all sorts of feelings mixed up in his mind. He experienced the bitter life of working people but also was warmly welcomed by them. While in the officialdom of human indifference people intrigue against each other. These sharp contrasts of life experiences inspired him to write something.

Afterwards Li Bai wrote a poem titled *Spending One Night in an Old Woman's Hut at the Foot of Mount Five Pines*. He described the condition about his lodging at the foot of Mount Five Pines and also expressed his gratitude to the old woman:

"I lodge under the Mount Five Pines,
 Lonely, I feel not quite at ease.
Peasants work hard in autumn old;
Husking rice at night, the maid's cold.
Wild rice is offered on her knees;
The plate in moonlight seems to freeze.
I'm overwhelmed with gratitude.
Do I deserve the hard-earned food?"

28 李白晚年求师的故事

李白晚年，政治上很不得志，他怀着愁闷的心情往返于宣城、南陵、歙县（在今安徽省）、采石矶等地，写诗饮酒，漫游名山大川。

一天清晨，李白像往日一样，在歙县城街头的一家酒店买酒，忽听隔壁的柴草行里有人在问话："老人家，你这么一大把年纪，怎么能挑这么多柴草，你家住哪儿？"回答的是一阵爽朗的大笑声。接着，便听见有人在高声吟诗："负薪朝出卖，沽酒日西归。借问家何处？穿云入翠微！"李白听

了，不觉一惊。这是谁？竟随口吟出这样动人的诗句！他问酒保，酒保告诉他：这是一位叫许宣平的老翁，他恨透了官府，看穿了世俗，隐居深山，但谁也不知道他住在哪座山里。最近，他常到这一带来游历，每天天一亮，就见他挑柴进镇，柴担上挂着花瓢和曲竹杖。卖掉柴就打酒喝，喝醉了就吟诗，一路走一路吟，过路的人还以为他是疯子呢。

李白暗想：这不是和自己一样的"诗狂"吗？他马上转身出门，只见那老翁上了街头的小桥，虽然步履艰难，但李白无论怎么赶也赶不上。

追上小桥，穿过竹林，绕过江汉（河流的分岔），李白累得气喘吁吁，腰酸腿痛，定神一看，老翁早已无影无踪了。李白顿足长叹："莫不是我真的遇上了仙人！"

他撩起袍子又赶了一程，还是不见老翁，只好失望地回来。

那天夜里，李白怎么也睡不着，回想起自己大半辈子除了杜甫之外，还没结识到几个真正的诗友。没想到今天竟遇上这样一个诗仙，可不能错过机会，一定要找到他！

第二天，李白在柴草行门口一直等到日落西山，也不见老翁踪迹。

第三天，第四天，天天落空。

第五天一早，李白背起酒壶，带着干粮上路了。他下了最大的决心，找不到老翁，就是死也要死在这儿的山林里。

翻过座座开满野花的山冈，蹚过道道湍急的溪流，拨开丛丛荆棘，整整一个多月，还是没见老翁的影子。李白有点泄气了。正在这时候，他回想起少年时碰到的那位用铁杵磨针的老婆婆，老婆婆说得好，"只要功夫深，铁杵磨成针"。要想找到老翁，就看自己有没有毅力啦。想到这里，李白紧紧腰带，咬咬牙，又往前走。累了，趴在岩石上睡一会；饿了，摘一把野果充饥；酒瘾上来，就捧着酒壶美美地喝上一口。

这天黄昏，晚霞把天空染得通红通红，清泉与翠竹互为衬托，显得分外秀丽。李白一心惦念着老翁，哪顾得欣赏景色。他拖着疲惫的身子，一瘸一拐地来到黄山附近的紫阳山下。转过山口，只见前面立着一块巨石，上面似乎还刻着字。李白忘记了疲劳，一头扑上去，仔细辨认起来，哦，原来是一首诗："隐居三十载，筑室南山巅。静夜玩明月，闲朝饮碧泉。樵夫歌垄上，谷鸟戏岩前。乐矣不知老，都忘甲子年。"

连读三遍，李白失声叫道："妙哉！妙哉！真是仙人之声哪！"心想：见到老翁，一定得拜他三拜，好好请教请教。虽说自己也跟诗打了几十年交道，但这散发着野花香味的诗还真是头回领略呢。

他回转身，看见崖石边的平地上摊着一堆稻谷，看来，准是许宣平老翁晒的。李白索性往边上一蹲，一边欣赏山中的景致，一边等老翁来收谷。

天黑了，李白忽听到山下传来阵阵击水声，循声望去，只见山下的小河对岸划来一只小船，一位须发飘飘的老人立在船头弄桨。李白上前询问道："老人家，请问，许宣平老翁家在何处？"原来这老人正是李白要找的许宣平老翁，上次他见李白身穿御赐锦袍，以为又是官家派来找他去做官的，所以再也不愿去歙县城了。没料到，此人竟跟踪而来。这时，老人瞟了李白一眼，随手指指船篙，漫不经心地答道："门口一杆竹，便是许翁家！"

李白抬眼望了望郁郁葱葱的山峦，又问："处处皆青竹，何处去找寻？"

老人重新打量着这位风尘仆仆、满脸汗水的客人，反问道："你是……"

"我是李白。"说着，李白深深地一揖。

老人愣住了："你是李白？李白就是你？"

李白连忙说明了自己的来意。老人一听，双手一拱："哎呀，你是当今的诗仙！我算什么，不过是诗海里的一滴水罢了。你这大海怎么来向一滴水求教，实在不敢当，不敢当！"说完，撑起船就要往回走。

李白一把拉住老翁的衣袖，苦苦哀求道："老人家，三个月了，我风风雨雨到处找你，好不容易见到了老师，难道就这样打发我回去不成！"

李白真挚的话语打动了老人的心。两人对视了好久，老人猛地拉住李白，跳上了小船。

从此，无论在漫天的朝霞里，还是在落日的余晖中，人们经常看到李白和这位老人，坐在溪水边的大青石上饮酒吟诗。那朗朗的笑声，和飞瀑的喧哗声汇成一片，随溪水一起送到百里千里之外……

至今，许多游人一到黄山，总爱顺着淙淙的溪水，去追寻李白的游踪。

看见了吗？过虎头岩，在鸣弦泉下，有一块刻着"醉石"二字的巨石，传说，当年李白和老人就在这里欣赏山景，饮酒吟诗。他们经常用旁边的泉水来洗酒杯，所以这泉就叫"洗杯泉"。

28 Li Bai Seeks Teacher in His Twilight Years

In his later years, Li Bai was politically unappreciated. Thereafter, he frequently traveled to Xuancheng, Nanling, She county (in present Anhui province) and Caishiji in a gloomy mood and indulged himself in drinking, writing and visiting famous mountains and rivers.

One morning, Li Bai bought wine from a wineshop in She county as usual. Suddenly, a voice came from the next firewood shop: "Grand old man, you are so old. How can you carry so much firewood? Where do you live?" A roar of laughter was heard in response. Then a poem reached his ears: "Selling firewood in the morning, returning with wine after the sundown. If you ask where my home is, it is located in the deep forest." Li Bai was surprised at someone blurting out such a good poem. So he asked the attendant, "Who is he?" The attendant answered: "His name is Xu Xuanping. Due to his dislike of the authorities and the secular world, he lived in seclusion in the mountains. And no one knows which mountain he lives in. Recently, he has been coming to this area. Regularly at day break he carries firewood to the town, with his wine pot and stick of bamboo hanging together in the firewood. After selling the firewood, he would usually buy wine. After drinking, he would chant poems. So passersby think he is a madman."

Li Bai thought: isn't he a poetic maniac like me? So he immediately turned around and walked out of the wineshop. Although he saw the old man trudging across a small bridge, he still couldn't catch up with him.

After crossing the bridge, bamboo forests and tributaries (the branches of the river), Li Bai got breathless and tired. When he had time to look around, the old man had gone out of sight. Li Bai stopped and sighed: "Have I really met an immortal?"

He lifted his robe and continued his chasing, but still couldn't see the old man. Finally, he came back with disappointment.

That night, Li Bai was sleepless. He recalled his experience of meeting Du Fu, but other than that he had made very few other true poetic friends. He didn't expect to meet such an immortal poet as that, so he must seize the opportunity to find him!

The next day, Li Bai waited at the gate of the firewood shop until sunset without seeing the old man.

He waited there on the third day, the forth day, but in vain.

Early on the fifth day, Li Bai was on his way with his wine pot and food. He decided that if he couldn't find the old man, he would rather die there.

During the whole month, he climbed mountains full of wild flowers, crossed swift streams and barbed thorns, but nowhere to see the old man. Li Bai grew a little discouraged when the story of the old woman grinding an iron rod into a needle occurred to him when he was a child. The story told him that "So long as you work hard enough, you can grind an iron rod into a needle—perseverance spells success". So he thought this must be a chance to test his persistence. Having adjusted his hat and clothes, he continued. When feeling tired, he would have a nap on a rock. When feeling hungry, he would pick berries to eat. And when wanting to drink, he would take a good drink from his wine pot.

One evening, everything looked particularly beautiful with the sunset glowing, tinting the sky red, and the spring and bamboo setting against each other. However, Li Bai was too preoccupied to appreciate the scene when thinking about the old man. He dragged his fatigued body, limping to the foot of Mount Ziyang near Mount Huang. Turning around the mountain pass, he saw a large stone engraved with some characters. Li Bai forgot his fatigue and immediately rushed to it and read it carefully. Oh, it was a poem: "Being in seclusion for thirty years, building home on the tops of the South Mountain. Appreciating the moon in quiet nights, and drinking the clear spring in day times. The farmer singing in the fields, the birds playing before the stones. I was too happy to remember the time, and almost forget my age."

After reading it for three times, Li Bai cried out: "Wonderful! That is excellent indeed! It must be written by an immortal!" And he thought that if he met the old man, he would implement worship ceremony, and ask him for advice; and that although he had composed poems for decades but had never seen a poem with a fresh wild flower fragrance before.

He turned around and saw a pile of rice lying on the flat ground beside the cliff. He thought it must be dried by the old man named Xu Xuanping. Li Bai squatted by it appreciating the view and waiting for the old man to collect rice.

At dusk, Li Bai suddenly heard the sound of water and saw an old man paddling a boat on the river. Li Bai stepped forward and asked: "Grand old man, Can you tell me how to get to the home of Xu Xuanping?" Actually the old man was Xu Xuanping. Last time he saw Li Bai wearing official suits, he thought this man was sent to ask him to serve in *yamen*. Indeed, Xu Xuanping didn't want to go She county again. But unexpectedly, the man followed him, so he shot a glance at Li Bai and pointed the fence without thinking: "Where there is a bamboo standing in doorway, there is Xu's home."

Li Bai looked at the verdant mountain and asked: "Green bamboo covers the whole mountain, where can I seek for him?"

The old man looked at the sweaty and tired guest again and asked: "You are...?"

"I'm Li Bai." he answered and bowed deeply.

The old man was stunned: "Are you Li Bai? Is it really you?"

Li Bai hurriedly explained his purpose. The old man bowed and said: "Ah, you are the immortal poet; compared with you, I am nobody, just like a drop of water in the sea in the poetical world. Why do you ask me for advice? You are flattering me! I'm not worthy of this!" With that, he approached his boat.

But Li Bai held his sleeves and begged: "Grand old man, I have been seeking you for three months. Finally I found you, how can you send me back?"

The old man was impressed by Li Bai's sincere words. They looked at each other for a while, the old man suddenly held Li Bai and jumped into the boat.

Since then, Li Bai and the old man were seen reciting poems and drinking on the big bluestone near the stream. Their laughter, together with the sound of waterfall, was carried thousands of *li* away with the stream.

Today, when visitors come here in Mount Huang, they often like to follow Li Bai's footsteps along the gurgling stream.

After crossing Tiger Rock, visitors can see a large stone engraved with "Drunk Stone" under the Mingxian Spring. It was said that Li Bai and the old man appreciated the mountain view, drinking and chanting poems there. They also used the spring to wash wine glasses, so the spring is called "Xi Bei Spring", which means glass-washing spring.

29 李白大义营救郭子仪的故事

"一代威名迈光弼，千秋知己属青莲。"这是一首咏史诗中评论唐朝名将郭子仪的诗句。意思是说，郭子仪的名气盖过了当时战功显赫的大将李光弼，他的知己则是大诗人李白。

李白与郭子仪之间的关系，有这样一个故事流传甚广。

传说故事中的李白颇具知鉴之能。郭子仪20岁的时候，曾在太原服役。因押运的粮草被烧，要以军法处置。在押赴刑场途中，正好遇上了李白。当时李白穿着玄宗皇帝恩赐的紫袍骑着玉龙大马遨游在长安大道上，忽见一簇刀斧手拥着一辆囚车行来。李白就停下马来问囚车中的人是谁，一问才知道原来是并州（今太原）押解到京城的将官，今押赴东市处斩，问其姓名，那人声如洪钟答道："姓郭名子仪。"李白见他容貌非凡甚是英伟，且临危不惧，认定他将来一定大有造化，日后必为国家柱石，就喝住刀斧手："待我亲往驾前保奏。"众人知是御前草诏御手调羹的李学士谁敢不依。李白回马直叩宫门，求见玄宗皇帝，讨了一道赦敕书，亲往东市开

读，打开囚车，救出郭子仪，许他戴罪立功。郭子仪后来果然不负所望，成了大将军，安史之乱爆发前，他已出任天德军使，兼九原太守、朔方节度右兵马使。郭子仪在安史之乱初期为国平乱，立下了赫赫战功。

安史之乱期间，李白因加入永王李璘幕下，涉嫌反叛唐肃宗，兵败后身陷囹圄。多亏已经功勋卓著的郭子仪得知这件事后出面解救，郭子仪甘愿以其官爵为李白赎罪，求见唐肃宗说："臣请求赦免李白。他确实无心谋反，实在是受了欺骗。"才得以使肃宗皇帝免李白死罪而流放夜郎。

这样，已经50多岁的李白，又开始了流放的生活。一路上，他心情悲伤，很少写诗。还没到达夜郎，又传来皇帝大赦的消息，李白可以不去夜郎了。他虽然获得了自由，可是须发已经变白了。

29 Li Bai Heroically Rescues Guo Ziyi

"His fame was beyond Guangbi, and his confidant is the buddhist Qinglian." This was the verse of one historical poem complimenting the famous general Guo Ziyi. It meant that the fame of Guo Ziyi was beyond that of general Li Guangbi whose battle achievement was remarkable, and his best friend was the great poet Li Bai.

There is a famous story about the relationship between Li Bai and Guo Ziyi.

It was said that Li Bai has the ability to identify talents. At the age of 20, Guo Ziyi served in military in Taiyuan. Because the provisions that he carried were burned, he would be punished by the military law. Fortunately, he met Li Bai on the way to the execution place. Li Bai wore an official suit wandering on the street of Chang'an riding on Yulong horse. Suddenly, he saw a group of executioners escorting a paddy wagon. So Li Bai stopped and asked what had happened. He learned that an official of Bingzhou (present Taiyuan) was to be executed in the east market. Li Bai asked his name, he answered loudly: "My name is Guo Ziyi." From his handsome looking and courage, Li Bai believed that Guo Ziyi would be a potential talent of the country. So Li Bai stopped those executioners and shouted: "I will go to ask Emperor Xuanzong for absolution for him." Those executioners stopped because they knew the story about the emperor and Scholar Li. Then Li Bai turned around and went straight to the emperor for absolution. After a moment, he went back and read the imperial edict in person, giving Guo Ziyi the chance to redeem himself by good service. As excepted, Guo Ziyi became a general with the post of truce envoy of Tiande, the Prefecture Chief of Jiuyuan, envoy of Shuofang before the An-shi Rebellion. He resisted the rebels and made outstanding military exploits during the revolt.

During the An-shi Rebellion, Li Bai was called to join in the loyal force led by Prince Yong—Li Lin. And he was convicted and detained in prison after the prince was defeated. Fortunately, distinguished Guo Ziyi knew the situation and wanted to save him at the cost of his official post. So Guo Ziyi interceded with Emperor Suzong for Li Bai, saying that Li Bai did not mean to rebel but was just deceived by others. Finally, Li Bai was exempted from death but banished to Yelang.

Thus, Li Bai, already in his fifties, started his life in exile. In a sad mood, he seldom wrote poems. On his half way to Yelang, news came of the emperor's amnesty that he didn't have to go there. Although he regained his freedom, his hair and beard turned white.

30 李白"千秋万岁名"称号的故事

天宝十四年（755年），安史之乱爆发，李白正在宣城、庐山一带隐居。次年十二月他怀着消灭叛乱、恢复国家统一的志愿应邀入永王李璘幕下。永王触怒肃宗被杀后，李白也因此获罪，被系浔阳（今江西九江）

狱，不久流放夜郎。途中遇赦得归，时已59岁。晚年流落在江南一带。当听到太尉李光弼率大军出镇临淮，讨伐安史叛军，李白不顾61岁的高龄，闻讯前往请缨杀敌，希望在垂暮之年，为挽救国家危亡尽力，因病中途返回。因为长期的漂泊生活和过量饮酒，李白成了体弱多病的老人，只好去投靠在当涂（在今安徽省）的族叔李阳冰。

秋天的一个早晨，李白起床以后，无意中瞧了镜子一眼，不禁大吃一惊，拿起镜子细照，只见镜中人非常憔悴衰老。

"唉!"李白深深地叹了一口气，有些悲伤地吟起诗来：

"自笑镜中人，白发如霜草。

扣心空叹息，问影何枯槁？"

九月九日重阳节，是个登高的节日。李白带病登上高坡，采来菊花饮酒。第二天，他又去采摘菊花，准备饮酒。只见菊花枝叶零落，不由见景生情，联想到自己一生所受的挫折和打击，又作了一首感伤的诗。

李白终于病倒了，不能外出。他让人扶他坐起来，拿过纸笔，用颤抖的手写下了"临终歌"三个字，又歇息了一会儿，才慢慢写起来：

"大鹏飞兮振八裔，中天摧兮力不济。

余风激兮万世，游扶桑兮挂左袂。

后人得之传此，仲尼亡兮谁为出涕!"

不久，一代大诗人李白辞别了人世。后世认为，此诗中李白所抒发的志向和悲愤之情，可看作他的墓志铭。

关于李白的死，民间流传着好几种说法。有人说他是醉酒去捞江中月而死。譬如，五代时的王定保在《唐摭言》中说："李白着宫锦袍，游采石江中，傲然自得，旁若无人，因醉入水中捉月而死。"始有李白狂醉捉月而死的首次记载。继后，北宋宣城人梅尧臣在《采石月下赠功甫》诗中又说："采石月下闻谪仙，夜披宫锦坐钓船。醉中爱月江底悬，以手弄月身翻然。"他把李白醉中弄月翻船而死说得更为形象。有人说他沿长江游览，这天，泊舟在采石江边。当晚月明如昼，李白坐在船头畅饮，忽然听见天边音乐之声嘹亮，而且越传越近。接着，江中风浪大作，有条几丈长的大鲸鱼，鼓起长须浮出水面，有两个仙童，手持旌节，来到李白面前，口称：

"天帝派我俩迎接星主还位。"舟上其他人都惊吓得昏死过去。待醒来时，只见李白坐在鲸背上，音乐前导，腾云驾雾升天去了。譬如，明代丘浚在《谪仙楼》一诗中写道："此翁自是太白精，星月相合自随行，当时落水非失脚，直驾长鲸归紫清。"说李白不是失足落水溺亡，是驾长鲸回归紫清宫了，如此等等。这些传说，表达了人们对李白的热爱。

千百年来，人们宁肯相信李白这位才华横溢、命运多舛的唐代伟大的浪漫主义诗人、诗仙加酒仙，是跨鲸背仙游羽化而去的。李白的诗歌对后代产生了深远的影响，虽然他活着的时候寂寞困苦，但他赢得了"千秋万岁名"的崇高评价。

30 The Origin of the Title "Long Live the Name Li Bai"

When the An-shi Rebellion broke out in the fourteenth year of Tianbao, Li Bai lived in seclusion in Xuancheng and Lushan. In the following December, with great aspirations to kill the rebels and reunify the nation, he joined the loyal forces led by Prince Yong—Li Lin, who was killed by enraged Emperor Suzong. Therefore, Li Bai was convicted and detained in Xunyang prison (in present Jiujiang, Jiangxi province). Finally, he was banished to Yelang. On his way to Yelang, he was exempted and released, but he was already 59 years old. He lived a wandering life in poverty in the areas of south Yangtze River in his later years. Despite being 61, he submitted a request for military service when he heard the news that Grand Commandant Li Guangbi would suppress the rebel forces, wanting to try his best to save his country from peril even in his declining years. But due to illness, he had to go back without achieving his goal. Since then, Li Bai became a feeble and sick old man because of his long drifting life and excessive drinking. Finally he had to fall back on his family uncle Li Yangbing in Dangtu (in present Anhui province).

One Autumn morning, Li Bai glanced at himself in the mirror unintentionally when he got up. He felt so surprised to find himself so gaunt and old.

"Alas!" Li Bai signed deeply and chanted poems sadly:

"Laugh at the man in the mirror, his grey hair is like the frosty grass.
To sigh with deep sorrow, why am I so old without vigor?"

September 9 in Chinese calendar, the Double Ninth Festival, is a traditional day for ascending. On that day, sick Li Bai ascended the mountain, picked chrysanthemum and drank wine. The next day, he planned to do the same thing again. However, the leaves and flowers began to wither and fall, which evoked his memories of the setbacks he had suffered throughout his life, so he wrote another sentimental poem.

Li Bai finally became sick and couldn't go out. He asked someone to help him sit up and pass him paper and writing brush, then he wrote *On Death Bed* with shaking hand. Resting for a while, he began to slowly write:

"When flies the roc he shakes the world,
In mid air his weakened wings are furled.
The wind he's raised still stirs the sea,
He hangs his left wing on sun-side tree.
Posterity mine, hear, O, hear!
Confucius dead, who'll shed a tear?"

Soon, great poet Li Bai passed away. The future generations thought this poem could be considered to be his epitaph because it expressed his ambition and grief.

In fact, there have been a number of theories about the death of Li Bai among people. One holds that he died when he fished the moon in the river after getting drunk. For instance, Wang Dingbao, a litterateur in the Five Dynasties, first recorded it in *Tang Chih-yen*: "Wearing an imperial brocade gown, Li Bai walked to the Caishi River. He was so proud that he acted as if nobody was around. Finally, he died because he fished the noon after getting drunk." Later, Mei Yaochen from Xuancheng in the Northern Song Dynasty described it in *To Gongfu in Midnight of Caishi*: "During the night, the immortal poet walked to Caishi; he was sitting in a boat with elaborate costumes. After drinking, he saw the bright moon in the river, so he tried to fish for it but slipped into the water." He gave a more vivid description of the death of Li Bai. And others said he liked to tour along the Changjiang River, and one night his boat moored alongside the Caishi River. Drinking on the bow in the bright moonlight, Li Bai suddenly heard the loud and clear sound of music from a distance drawing closer and closer. Then, rough wind sprang up, several big whales with long barbells came to the surface, and two fairy children took the credit and said to Li Bai, "God sends us to meet you, the Lord of Star." People on the boat were shocked to faint. When they woke up, they saw Li Bai sitting on the back of a whale, going up by the music into the heaven. For instance, Qiu Jun of the Ming Dynasty wrote it in *Taibai Floor*: "As the reincarnation of the Great White Planet Venus, the star always stays with the moon. He didn't slip down into the water, he went to the heaven by riding on a whale." It meant that Li Bai didn't slip into the water, but he just returned to the Ziqing Palace riding on a whale, etc. All these legends expressed people's love for Li Bai.

For thousands of years, people would rather believe that this brilliant and ill-fated great romanticist, poet immortal and wine immortal had ascended to heaven riding on the back of a whale and become immortal. Li Bai's poets have exerted a far-reaching influence on later generations and won him a reputation of "Long Live the name Li Bai".